BACK WHEN YOU
WERE EASIER TO LOVE

Back When You Were Easier to Love

Emily Wing Smith

DUTTON BOOKS

An imprint of Penguin Group (USA) Inc.

DUTTON BOOKS

A MEMBER OF PENGUIN GROUP (USA) INC.

Published by the Penguin Group | Penguin Group (USA) Inc., 375 Hudson Street, New York, New York 10014, U.S.A. | Penguin Group (Canada), 90 Eglinton Avenue East, Suite 700, Toronto, Ontario M4P 2Y3, Canada (a division of Pearson Penguin Canada Inc.) | Penguin Books Ltd, 80 Strand, London WC2R 0RL, England | Penguin Ireland, 25 St Stephen's Green, Dublin 2, Ireland (a division of Penguin Books Ltd) | Penguin Group (Australia), 250 Camberwell Road, Camberwell, Victoria 3124, Australia (a division of Pearson Australia Group Pty Ltd) | Penguin Books India Pvt Ltd, 11 Community Centre, Panchsheel Park, New Delhi - 110 017, India | Penguin Group (NZ), 67 Apollo Drive, Rosedale, North Shore 0632, New Zealand (a division of Pearson New Zealand Ltd) | Penguin Books (South Africa) (Pty) Ltd, 24 Sturdee Avenue, Rosebank, Johannesburg 2196, South Africa | Penguin Books Ltd, Registered Offices: 80 Strand, London WC2R 0RL, England

This book is a work of fiction. Names, characters, places, and incidents are either the product of the author's imagination or are used fictitiously, and any resemblance to actual persons, living or dead, business establishments, events, or locales is entirely coincidental.

The publisher does not have any control over and does not assume any responsibility for author or third-party websites or their content.

Library of Congress Cataloging-in-Publication Data
Smith, Emily Wing, date.-
Back when you were easier to love / by Emily Wing Smith.—1st ed.   p. cm.   Summary: When her boyfriend Zan leaves high school in Utah a year early to attend Pitzer College, a brokenhearted Joy and Zan's best friend Noah take off on a road trip to California seeking "closure."
ISBN 978-0-525-42199-3 (hardcover)   [1. Interpersonal relations—Fiction. 2. Mormons—Fiction. 3. Conduct of life—Fiction. 4. Automobile travel—Fiction. 5. Universities and colleges—Fiction.]   I. Title. PZ7.S646575Bac 2010   [Fic]—dc22   2010013469

Published in the United States by Dutton Books, a member of Penguin Group (USA) Inc.
345 Hudson Street, New York, New York 10014   www.penguin.com/youngreaders

Designed by Abby Kuperstock
Printed in USA | First Edition | 10 9 8 7 6 5 4 3 2 1

To Cammen—my Mattia, always

BACK WHEN YOU
WERE EASIER TO LOVE

HOW I SPENT
MY SUMMER VACATION

Over the summer my best friend, Mattia, and I were the token teenage patrons of Haven Public Library. I guess all the other kids figured that since we were out of school, it meant we were exempt from "required reading" which, in their minds, meant any reading at all.

Honestly, I think Mattia went less because she liked to read and more because she liked to make fun of a library with a set of encyclopedias claiming that Hawaii had yet to become a state. We would mock the skimpy selection of bestsellers and pore over the card catalog because the handful of computers in the place were always down.

But I loved the library simply because it was a library. I love libraries. I like reading, but I love libraries. Being surrounded by books makes me feel safe, the way some people need trees or mountains around them to feel secure. Not me—nature's not what I cling to. I cling to books.

Books have always been there, whether as copies of Aristotle and Hegel lining my philosophy-professor father's office walls or volumes of *This Fabulous Century* shoved into random closets for my social-history-obsessed mother. Some people remember their life in landscapes. I remember mine in titles.

Of course I'd never admit it to anyone, but the aspect of the Haven Public Library I found most fascinating was the bulletin board. The entire back wall was covered in corkboard, and it was plastered with flyers detailing community announcements.

I loved reading about what was for sale. "Antique" wicker rockers. Some kid's old teddy bear selling for thirty-seven dollars (or best offer). My favorite: a 1977 Impala that ran "like new." That ad has been up ever since I moved to Haven nine-and-a-half months ago.

But more than I liked the for-sale section, more than I liked the help-wanted posters, I liked the Calendar of Events.

One event on the calendar that dry August afternoon was the workshop "Grief and the Adolescent." I knew as soon as I read it that this workshop was created specifically to help me through my time of need. I continued reading the description. Had I become lonely? *Check.* Despondent? *More often than I wanted to admit.* Did I want to feel a sense of closure and inner peace? *Obviously.*

"Mattia," I said, jabbing her in the ribs, "look at this."

She stared at it, puzzled. "But you don't have any chil-

dren. Why would you need to attend a parenting class?"
She faked concern. "There isn't anything you need to tell
me, is there?"

"Not that," I said. "The one next to it."

Mattia started to read again. After a long moment, she
looked up. "Yeah, I can see how you might think that
could help you." She paused. "I know you miss him. But
Joy, Zan didn't die."

THE LUNCHROOM, NOW

Now it's the end of September. Daytime highs are still over a hundred degrees. My boyfriend is no closer to home than he was back then.

I'm sick of this school already. At first I thought I'd stop hating the maze of unlabeled hallways once I figured them out. I thought I'd learn to love the clean, Disneyland-style environment. I thought I'd get used to Haven High's unique brands of cliquedom: the all-female Color Guard, the all-male A Cappella Singers, the ultrapopular Soccer Lovin' Kids.

Without Zan, none of this is worth it.

Everything seems exactly the same as it was last year: gross plastic furniture in bright, awkward colors; the smell of fried food and antiseptic; insanely long lines. An outsider wouldn't notice Zan's not being here, but it changes the whole feel of this place. I slump down into an orange chair.

"Noah was asking about you again in calculus," says Mattia. She drops to our lunch table, holding a slice of pizza and a carton of Tampico. "It's getting pretty stalker-esque, Joy. You should talk to him."

"No thanks." The cafeteria is already crowded, and I scan the faces. I don't know who I'm looking for. On the surface I'd say Charlotte, or Kristine, but deep down I'm longing to see Zan, longing to breathe again at the familiarity of his not-quite smile.

Over Mattia's shoulder I spot a group of perky sophomores a few tables over. One of them is standing up, and her T-shirt has MODEST IS HOTTEST silk-screened across the front.

Maybe Zan wouldn't have left if the girls here didn't wear *Modest Is Hottest* T-shirts.

The sophomores burst into giggles; each of their smiles could be on a dental brochure for capping or bonding. "Girls with yellow teeth don't stand a chance at this school," I say, mainly to myself. "Is teeth-bleaching mandatory on this campus?"

Maybe Zan wouldn't have left if my teeth were whiter.

"Hey, guys." Charlotte sets her tray on our table carefully: an apple, green beans, spaghetti, and skim milk. Very balanced; very Charlotte. "Kristine's still in line," she says, then glances at me. "Where's your lunch?"

"Not hungry," I tell her.

She and Mattia share a glance.

"Eating disorder," Mattia says to me, like it's a threat.

7

THE LUNCHROOM, THEN

I remember the first time I saw Alexander Kirchendorf. My heart has never stopped like that, before or since. It was one moment, that fast. Second lunch my second day at Haven. I was sitting, giggling with Mattia and Kristine, pretending to be happy. I don't remember what we were discussing, but I saw him and stopped talking, stopped listening.

He was sitting with his best friend, Noah, playing cards. And maybe it was the way the light from the windows hit his hair, making it look like satin. Maybe it was his eyes, eyes like chocolate pudding—the real kind—cooked over a stove until it almost boils.

But I think it was his smile. On that day, that day during second lunch on my second day at Haven High, I didn't know just how rare a thing a smile from Alexander Kirchendorf was. But he smiled that day, that moment, because he had just won again. His teeth were perfect.

I could find myself in that smile, and that's what I needed then—finding. So I knew it, like you know it when you're getting strep throat. You can't feel the full effect yet, but you know it's unavoidable; that it will get much worse before it gets better.

I am infatuated by intellect. I fall for smart guys the way other girls fall for athletic guys or surfer guys, tall guys or blond guys. I fell in love with Zan, and maybe it was because he spoke fluent Esperanto that I was hooked. Or because he wrote my name in Tengwar, and it looked so exotic. Part of it was to spite the conventional Haven High crowd, who thought his habit of wearing khakis with tucked-in polo shirts was weird, not endearing. And he wore these old brown loafers, his grandfather's shoes.

Zan wanted to be a linguistics professor at Berkeley and head up studies and publish in prestigious journals. He wanted the inner-city Northern California lifestyle: good public transportation, cheap Thai food, Telegraph Avenue, the whole shebang. He'd get it, too: he was ambitious like that. He would write me poetry in Estar, his constructed language. He'd put the translation in the margin.

Estar was like a code, and only together could we crack it.

HOW I MET MATTIA

I moved to Haven midyear, midsemester, mid-everything, including my life.

First impressions are usually right, and I got a pretty accurate sense of Haven High walking in to register. It smelled way too clean, for one, a weird fake-clean. There was Matchbox 20 music playing over the loudspeaker, so it felt like Rob Thomas was following you everywhere you went. The weirdest part was the smiley faces. They were hand-drawn on shiny yellow paper and taped all over the school.

"Are those here all the time?" I asked Mr. Daniel, pointing at one above the copy machine.

"Hmm?" he said, grabbing my schedule off the printer tray. He handed it to me and looked up where I was pointing. "Oh, no, those are for Happiness Week." He said it like it was obvious this random week in January was made to celebrate happiness. Or encourage happiness. I'm still not sure about the actual point of Happiness Week.

"The layout of this school is pretty confusing," he said, which I had already noted while trying to get to his office. "That's why we give new students a Husky Ambassador to show them around the first couple of days."

The whole Husky Ambassador thing sounded like a pretty humiliating setup, both for me and my ambassador. She was to show me around the school, take me to and pick me up from my classes, and even eat lunch with me until, apparently, after two days I made my own friends.

I also didn't get the hard-core mascot love at HHS. Mr. Daniel had given me a list of extracurricular activities, including a drill team called the "Pup Club" and some school-spirit program called the "Iditarod." But calling the ambassadors husky was a low blow.

Mattia, it turned out, wasn't husky. She wasn't embarrassed by her position, either. "This is the good bathroom," she said, on our official Welcome Tour. "The rest don't have doors for some reason. The SBOs are working on changing that."

"Doors to the stalls?" I asked, disgusted. Now *there* was a lawsuit waiting to happen. And what were SBOs?

Mattia shook her head. "No, just doors going into the bathroom, thank goodness." I liked the way Mattia talked quaint, but straightforward.

"On the left is the library. No one ever goes in there, but if you do, watch out for the librarian. Even the teachers don't like him. This vending machine is more expensive than the one upstairs, so avoid it. The sign on that blue-and-white locker says NOTES FOR THE BIG DOG. It's like a suggestion box. I don't know if anybody reads them or not, because no students have the combination. So it might be the administration's way of pretending like we actually have a say in anything." She exhaled. "Okay, so any questions?"

I shook my head.

"Don't worry, Joy." She smiled at me—not fake. "It's going to be okay."

MEANWHILE, BACK IN
THE "REAL" WORLD

According to books, movies, and TV shows, high schools give students school-sanctioned time for study hall—sitting in the library or an empty classroom and passing notes or painting nails or cramming for tests.

At Haven High, giving students this kind of freedom would give the faculty a collective heart attack. Here, there is no study hall. Home is for studying. School is for superstructured lessons.

I could live with that, back when I liked nothing better than studying in the serenity of my bedroom. I would sit at my desk and breathe in the calm and essence of intellect that lingered from that first day he was there. When I'm in my room now, just opening a textbook makes me hurt.

Homework has to get done somehow, though, which is how I get resigned to spending the remainder of my lunch period in the library. Truthfully, I don't mind. "Sorry, guys," I say, and check my watch for good measure, "I have some AP bio to finish up."

"Want help?" asks Charlotte, cutting her spaghetti. We're lab partners.

I shake my head. "Thanks, but I'm good. See you in class, okay?"

The library's almost always deserted. I mean, seriously—it has a rude librarian, decades-old books, and no computers. Who'd want to hang there?

I take my usual table near the fat atlas.

I'm already deep into the textbook/work sheet groove, searching my backpack for my pink highlighter, when I see it. It's tucked in the folds of fabric at the bottom of the bag, hidden to the untrained eye. But I see it. I know what's printed on the pencil even before I pick it up: MISS THORPE THINKS YOU'RE SPECIAL. Gold lettering.

Swallow the scream, Joy. Swallow it.

MISS THORPE THINKS
YOU'RE SPECIAL

Mattia refused to believe it when I told her Zan had come over to my house exactly three afternoons after the initial sighting. "Zan *Kirchendorf*?" She specified, as though Haven High was crawling with Zans, particularly ones I would invite to my house. Her head shook hard enough that her waist-length, tawny-blond hair shook along with it. "Zan doesn't go to girls' houses. Zan doesn't hang out. That's not how he is."

But that's how he was with me.

"I hear you're pretty good at French," I'd told him. An understatement. He was fluent, knew more than the teacher. "I'm horrible at it," I continued. Not an understatement. "Maybe you could give me some pointers?"

"You're new here, right?" Zan gave me that smile, the one that first hooked me, the one that untied all the knots in the shoelace inside me. "Joy, you said your name was?"

I hadn't said, which meant he'd been asking about me like I'd been asking about him, which meant it was supposed to happen when he said, "How about I come over tomorrow after school?" and then he did.

When Zan arrived I was unpacking books. Under normal circumstances a girl would stop unpacking books when a guy came by, but these weren't normal circumstances; these were our circumstances. I told him I was unpacking books, and he asked if he could help, and I led him to my new bedroom. Technically, I wasn't allowed to have guys in my bedroom, but my parents still owed me big-time for moving us to Haven, and I decided this would help them pay me back.

The two empty ladder-style bookcases gave my room a bare look, even though I already had a white desk with a pink Sony laptop and a bed made with linens from the Target designer I liked. I'd purposely waited until last to unpack my books. I loved my books too much to shove on a shelf willy-nilly. Books equaled permanence.

I was still working to convince myself this surreal Haven-existence was permanent.

Zan knelt over an open box of books, running his finger down the spines. His lips weren't smiling, but his eyes were. He was wearing the loafers. And he sorted books the way I did: fiction by author's last name; nonfiction by Dewey decimal. Not many people do that.

The shelves were nearly full, and I was organizing my

old *Junie B. Jones* collection according to publication date. Zan started laughing. Quiet at first, then louder.

"What?" I looked over his shoulder, getting close enough to breathe in the smell of him. He had that good, washed-boy smell. He wore his grandpa's shoes, but not his aftershave. He spoke European languages, but didn't practice European hygiene. He was the best of everything absurd. "Why are you laughing?"

He didn't answer, but he didn't need to. I could see. "That's my 'special box,'" I said, defensive. "It doesn't need to be unpacked." I tried to put the lid back on, but Zan lightly pushed me away. "What's a special box?" he asked.

"A box of special things," I said. "Duh."

"Special things like writing instruments that tell you how special you are?" A smile tugged at Zan's lips. He was holding a "pencil bouquet," from my second-grade teacher. The six pencils were each a different color, with gold lettering: MISS THORPE THINKS YOU'RE SPECIAL.

"I was in second grade!" I plucked out a green one. "Didn't people tell you how special you were when you were seven years old?"

"Sure," he said. "Lots of people did. But it didn't mean anything. Lots of people tell everybody they're special here. That's what this town is—a bunch of Mormons go- ing around thinking they're special, because since they're

Mormon they know how the world's supposed to work." He looked up at me. "In case you're curious, the world's supposed to be just like Haven."

I nodded, because I'd already noticed that. People had a disbelief that places could exist where it was normal to see grocery stores selling wine and copies of *Cosmo* that weren't hidden behind thick plastic "modesty screens." Maybe it wasn't a disbelief that these places existed, as much as a disbelief that someone would want to live in such a den of iniquity.

"But if the world becomes just like Haven," I began— I looked into Zan's huge eyes, stared into them without a hint of self-consciousness, and I smiled—"then Haven won't be special anymore."

"Exactly! It's like putting everything you've ever owned into your special box."

"Well, I think you're special." I tucked the pencil behind his ear, pushing back shiny, feathered hair. "And I don't say that to just anyone."

He picked a red pencil from the bouquet. "Neither do I," he said, handing it to me.

Maybe this surreal Haven-existence was permanent.

But Zan was permanent, too.

LISTEN: DO YOU WANT TO KNOW A SECRET?

I *have never* been popular.

Not that I'm popular now. But I'm more popular than a girl who transferred to a clique-ridden high school nine months ago has any right to be. I know that. I know I'm lucky. I don't feel lucky, but I know I am.

It was moving from the outside world that did it. Nobody knew that Claremont was just another boring city. Nobody knew that my thick brown hair that happened to be stylish in Haven wasn't stylish anywhere else. Nobody knew that it only *seemed* like I was supersmart because I'd already studied *The Great Gatsby*. Nobody knew that back home I'd had exactly three friends, including my best friend, Gretel. And I'd grown up with her, so she more or less had to hang out with me. Nobody knew how uncomfortable I felt around popular kids, always like the one at the birthday party someone's mom made them invite. Nobody knew I'd never been kissed.

People assumed I was a sophisticated city girl, and I let them believe it because I thought they'd figure out the truth soon enough.

Sometimes I think only one of them did.

OF BEVERAGE NIGHT
AND BEST FRIENDS

I hear a voice from somewhere over my shoulder. "Biology, huh? May I be of service?"

I shake the crumbs out of my head and look over into the face of Noah Talbot: blue-eyed, wide-smiled, completely delusional Noah Talbot.

For once, Mattia wasn't exaggerating: this *is* getting pretty stalker-esque. Noah and I don't talk. We aren't friends. Zan left us both, and apparently, Noah thinks that means we have to have some kind of meaningful conversation.

But I don't. Noah is king of the Soccer Lovin' Kids—Haven High's quintessential Golden Boy. He's athletic enough to be on the varsity soccer team, smart enough to be in AP classes, and spiritual enough to make being Mormon cool. He even *looks* golden, with hair the color of sand when it's hot, all shimmery-gold. His skin is naturally bronze even now, when summer is supposed to be over.

Most girls like Golden Boys, but they agitate me the way all popular kids do.

"Seriously," he says. "I'm really good in this class."

"Yeah?" I know I shouldn't say it, but it's too easy. "Do you know the average number of sperm in an ejaculation?"

I stare straight at him, and he starts rapid-fire blinking while his face grows pink. "Uh, I can't remember."

"Then you can't help me. Thanks, though."

Instead of walking away, Noah pulls a chair up to my table—another orange plastic one—and spins it backward before sitting down. "Listen, I've been trying to talk to you all week."

"Yeah, I heard. What's unclear to me is why."

"Last night was Beverage Night. This week it was at my house, and I wanted to invite you. Maybe next time?"

What is *wrong* with this guy? You can't even pick a fight with him. "Beverage Night?" I repeat.

"Yeah. We have it every Thursday as an alternative to all the lame school clubs we didn't want to join. It's evolved into true greatness. We've made our own root beer, and another time we made smoothies, and last night we made stuff from this cookbook called *101 Drinks You Can Make with Sprite*. A lot of them had alcohol so we had to substit—"

"Right, right, I get it." I put down my pencil. *Miss*

Thorpe Thinks You're Special. Once, Zan did, too. "So let me get this straight. Your big screw you to Haven High society at large is *Beverage Night*?"

"Well, I wouldn't have chosen those words." Noah's voice is calm and even.

My arms are folded on the table, and my head sinks onto them, face-first. Breathe. Raise head. Speak calmly. Match his tone. "Don't you get it? This is your fault. This is why Zan left. Beverage Night. MODEST IS HOTTEST T-shirts. Libraries that suck."

"Hey, I had nothing to do with the libraries." Noah puts out his hands palms-first, all innocence. "Don't blame me for that."

"But I can blame you for everything else? Because just so you know, I do. You were his best friend here . . . his *only* friend here. Couldn't you have eased up on the whole Mr. Haven Embodied thing? So he didn't have to completely rebel? So he didn't have to leave this place immediately?"

"Wait." Noah actually waits, like he's thinking something over. "You think it's because of me that Zan got his GED, skipped his senior year, and went to school in California? Have you *met* Zan? You of all people should know that he doesn't factor anyone else into his decisions."

"I just know what it's like when your friends don't

understand you. It makes you want to find people who do."

"Maybe you're right, okay?" Noah looks more serious than I've ever seen him. Although, that's not saying much. "Maybe I didn't understand him. That's what he had you for."

"Maybe I wasn't enough!" The words burn leaving my mouth. I'm surprised a tear is forming in the corner of my left eye. I am not sad. I am mad.

Mr. Jasper, the librarian, taps his meterstick against the checkout counter and glares at me, putting his finger to his lips and wiggling his eyebrows like "Be quiet!"

"This is not what I came here to talk about." Noah speaks in a whisper, and Mr. Jasper nods at him approvingly. Everyone approves of Noah. I am the only person in this school, this town, this world, who doesn't.

I look at him expectantly. "Then why *did* you come here?"

"I'm just trying to be your friend. Let me be your friend."

I hate it when people say they're trying to be your friend. You shouldn't have to *try* to be somebody's friend. Either you like someone or you don't. Either you want them as a friend or not. Making friends isn't like trying for the lead in the school play.

"Noah, can't you just leave me alone?" That's what seeing him reminds me of. Zan leaving me. Alone.

"Sorry," he says, not sounding sorry in the least. "We are going to be friends. That's how Zan would have wanted it."

He makes it sound like Zan's dead. "How do you know?"

"He told me," says Noah. He shrugs. "I promised, Joy. Don't make this harder than it already is. I promised."

JOY 2.0

I never got it, those magazine articles I read when I was thirteen and anticipating romance. Never understood why they went on and on about finding a guy you could be yourself around. I could be me all by myself. I was *already* me. I wanted a boyfriend to make me more than me.

Zan was that guy. Zan was that guy, and more. I wasn't myself with him, I was *better* than myself—Joy 2.0. When I was with Zan my jokes were funnier, my mind was sharper, my vanilla perfume smelled better. I was better read—quotes from books jumped into my memory during conversations with him.

With him, the world changed. Music was more intense—chords were stronger, old beats felt new, and lyrics were good again. Food tasted better. I didn't need as much of it because every bite had twice as much flavor, twice as many nutrients.

Before, I had to fight to fall asleep. Once I met Zan, sleep came quickly, flowing through the night, deep and dreamless. Before, I woke exhausted in the morning, the concept of rest baffling me. Once I met Zan, I awoke full of energy, my heart pounding, not out of fear but anticipation.

Without him, the world is smaller. Without him, I am smaller. Without him a place like Haven, a place that was small before, shrinks to the size of a fingernail clipping—something so small, something no one needed anyway.

I am not Haven. I shrink without Zan. But with him, I am not insignificant.

SUPER-SATURDAY

Super-Saturday *was* a Haven tradition. The white brick Mormon church on Nola Drive, built by pioneers and renovated about a dozen times since, hosted the annual event. It was a day-long extravaganza where mothers and daughters bonded over miniscrapbooks and fabric paints.

"I don't do crafts," I told Mattia.

"Everyone does crafts," said Mattia, rolling her eyes. "We'll sign you up for something supereasy, like spring-themed fingertip towels. Trust me, even an untrained ape could make those."

"No."

She kept talking. "You'll love it—it's such a good way to get rid of the winter blahs. I'm making a way cute magnet board with this polka-dotted ribbon on the—"

My look was strong enough to silence her.

"Okay," she said, ducking her head. "You can help in the nursery."

I actually didn't mind nursery duty. As one of the rare

Mormon girls without any siblings, I had always jumped at opportunities to watch the little kids while the church held Valentine's Day Dinner-Dances or had guest speakers and a potluck dinner for adults only. I'd open the nursery toy closet and dump assorted blocks and board books out of their plastic bins. The kids and I would play hangman on the chalkboard. I'd feed them graham crackers and pretzel bites.

I was the first babysitter at the church on Super-Saturday. I unlocked the toy closet and weeded through the toys, throwing away broken stuff and matching up the underwear-clad dress-up doll with her various felt outfits. Soon moms started dropping off their kids—mainly boys, or girls too young for the Super-Saturday festivities.

"I'll make you a flower barrette," one mom promised a clingy toddler. "But you have to be good."

Bribery by barrette. Only in Haven.

Pretty soon we had a full house, and I was managing nicely. One group was racing Hot Wheels on a homemade vinyl mat with little streets and parking lots drawn on it. A four-year-old was playing the minikeyboard with her little brother. I was regulating a dull game of Red Light/ Green Light with everybody else.

It was only when a girl in pink-sequined shoes asked me to take her to the bathroom that I realized something: I was all alone.

Where was everybody else? *Was* there an everybody else? I checked the standard-issue wall clock. Super-Saturday was well underway.

So I did the only thing I could think of: I texted Zan. *Wanna help me babysit? It's dire!*

What about your friends?

They're at Super-Saturday. I'm alone. Help! Church on Nola Drive.

He was there six minutes later. I knew I'd woken him because his hair was still wet and his chin and upper lip were stubbly. "Hey," he said, sounding tired.

"Be right back," I said, running out of the room holding hands with sequin-shoes. "I'm taking Trina to the potty." I whirled back around. "I mean, I'm taking her to the restroom."

Zan's lips hinted at a smile. "Go. I'll take care of things here."

Sometimes, lonely times, I replay those words in my head, the way I replayed them out loud that morning. "Yeah. You take care of things here."

BACK WHEN YOU WERE
EASIER TO LOVE

I have an exceptionally large bladder, so usually it's easy to avoid the school bathrooms. Today there's no way around it: the girls' room is the only place I can go where Noah won't follow me. The fluorescent light bouncing off the pink-tiled walls practically gives me a seizure, so I lock myself in the nearest stall.

There's zero actual graffiti anywhere on school premises, because whenever students get more than three tardies in one term, they have to "work them off" by cleaning the school for two hours. It's common to see a kid from your French class scrubbing garbage cans while you're heading out to the parking lot after school. The bathroom stalls are usually sparkling, according to Mattia, who has cleaned them more than once.

But while I'm standing in the stall, waiting for my eyes to adjust, I see something written on the top corner. There, in black Sharpie, are small letters—too deliberate for your run-of-the-mill vandalism. *Back when you were easier to love.*

Blink.

When did loving me become so hard?

Blink.

Why did loving me become so hard?

Blink. Blink.

What did he want me to be that I wasn't?

I can be that girl again. But I need him, first.

FABULOUS

My first date with Zan was to a gay-rights rally on Super-Saturday.

After the crafting died down and moms and big sisters came to collect, and after Zan and I put away the slobbery, broken toys, I was sure I'd never see him again. Not because I hadn't had fun.

I had. Kids loved Zan. Zan, who wore old-man shoes and had probably never played with a toy in his life. He talked quietly, and kids dropped their own voices to hear him. They laughed easily with him. They touched his no-time-to-shave stubble and he let them.

I'd had fun. But I wasn't sure Zan had.

"There's a poetry reading in about an hour, at the library," he said. "Want to go?"

I didn't want to feel anything but excitement, didn't want to feel anything but giddiness. Zan still liked me. Zan liked me even more, maybe. Zan was asking me out on a real date.

But I couldn't help the puzzlement crawling in my

mind. "The library?" I was thinking a poetry reading at Haven Public Library would yield exactly six people, all of them related to the poet.

He caught my meaning, of course. "The city library. Downtown."

The reading was by the poet laureate of some state back east, who had won a poetry prize I didn't want to let Zan know I'd never heard of before. For him, I wanted to be smarter than I really was.

So we took off, me in jeans with sticky fingerprints on the legs and Zan in a T-shirt with Latin all over the front that translated into: *If you can read this, you're overeducated.*

It was still light out, that glinty, glary late-winter-afternoon light that always deceived me into thinking it would last longer than it actually did. Winter days: reminders of how something so bright can fade so quickly.

Street parking was free after four on weekends, and Zan wedged his car into a space behind the library. The downtown library was one of my favorite buildings ever, and as I walked toward the front doors I kept my eyes upward, staring at the angular glass walls, jutting just-so to make the most of the lingering light.

When I bumped against someone I apologized instinctively, not realizing until I looked around that it wasn't just one person I'd run into—it was a whole bunch of people blockading the sidewalk.

34

"What's going on?" I asked, craning my neck. I could see now that the road between the library and City Hall was caution-taped off, and a cop was directing pedestrian traffic.

"I think it's a protest," said Zan, his eyes lighting up. "See the news vans?" He motioned to a woman with neat hair and a too-big microphone, standing next to a white van with the name of a local TV channel across it.

"Cool!" I grabbed Zan's hand, a risky move I was only now willing to make, now that the crowds were heavy. I wanted to get mixed up in them. I wanted to become one of the people with a cause, not one of the people who did crafts and babysat.

His hand was warm against my cold one, and I tightened my grip. "Come on!" I said, pulling him into the crowd. I wanted to lose myself, but I didn't want to lose him.

"You want to check this out?" Zan said into my ear as we ran across the street, zigzagging through groups of people. He sounded surprised.

"This might be my only chance to be in a protest march," I said. "And I want to make the world a better place."

"You realize this is a gay rights rally, don't you?" He dropped my hand and pointed upward.

I looked through the bare tree branches at a sign: WE ARE ALL EQUAL. Zan raised an eyebrow at me.

"We *are* all equal." I pulled together the two sides of my jacket and fumbled with a button. "And health-care rights for gay couples in this state are a joke."

His eyebrow arched higher. "Oh, really?"

"What, you don't agree?" I was trying to get my stupid button through the buttonhole without taking my eyes off Zan. Zan, with his thick, soulful eyebrows crinkled in thought, his big eyes, his two-day stubble pronounced against his pale skin.

"I'm just surprised," he said. "Not a lot of Mormons think about things like that."

"Not a lot of Mormons in *Haven* think about things like that," I said. My fingers were too cold now, and my button still wasn't done up.

"You really think it's different anywhere else?" His voice hadn't changed, not really, but there was a certain challenge in his tone. "In California the Church thinks gay marriage is hunky-dory?"

I rolled my eyes. "You *know* that's not what I mean. But at least for California Mormons gay marriage is actually an issue. Here, gay marriage is wrong, sinful, never-gonna-happen, period. There's no real debate. Just cold, midwinter protests that won't do any good." I blew on my hands, the warmth spreading fingertip to palm. "But I want to be a part of it anyway."

Zan nodded. "I do, too." He glanced at my coat, motioned toward it. "May I?" Before I could nod, he was buttoning it, starting at the bottom, fingers moving nimbly to the top. His eyes met mine. "Warmer now?"

I still couldn't nod, or speak, but I knew he knew. That I was warmer, that I wasn't like the other Haven girls. That I was in love, and he was falling for me, too. I knew he knew I knew all these things, in just one glance.

"That one, there," I said, regaining control of my body. "That's the best sign here." I walked toward it, and Zan followed like I knew he would.

The guy holding it was just a guy, just a youngish man in a blue parka standing there alone, apparently not affiliated with any group pro or anti. He was just a plain, ordinary guy with a sign in rainbow lettering: I SUPPORT THE RIGHT TO BE FABULOUS.

"I love your sign!" I told him.

He and Zan nodded at each other, maybe exchanging a look over my enthusiasm, but I didn't care. "We should find a reporter or something, because seriously, this sign says it all." True, I might have said it loud enough for the nearby reporter to overhear. So what? It got her attention, didn't it?

The reporter was identical to the first one we'd seen— same sleek hair, same sleek suit. She asked us a few questions and her photographer arranged us around the sign, like he was taking a family portrait.

The picture never made it into the paper, not that I saw at least. But the image in my mind is sharper than a newsprint photo could ever be. In my mind I see that prenight sun lighting us up from behind, making Zan glow, making me glow.

With him, being fabulous wasn't just a right. It was a privilege.

THE WORLD ACCORDING
TO HAVEN HIGH

Mr. Daniel's office is decorated in a style that falls somewhere between the Hard Rock Café and the tail end of a car. I stare at a poster that says "God could only make so many perfect heads—the rest he covered with hair!"

"You wanted to see me?" I hand him the note one of the office aide kids just delivered to my last-period class. I hate this day. I don't want to be living this day. I want Zan.

"Yes, sit, please." Mr. Daniel sifts through my file page by page then looks up at me.

"So." His face is earnest. "Where do you want to go from here?"

There's no real answer to a question like that, and Mr. Daniel doesn't care, anyway. He's all about catchphrases, like "keep your options open" and "anything is possible," but he knows little about the actual workforce and even less about post-secondary education. College counseling here is a joke. If a school is out-of-state or doesn't have a big-name football team, it might as well not exist.

To say I don't take this guy seriously doesn't even begin to describe it.

"Where do I want to go from here? I'm still trying to come to grips with the fact that I *am* here."

"Don't tell me you still haven't adjusted to life at Haven?" Mr. Daniel has been my counselor since I moved here and became the dreaded New Girl. He's always calling me into his office to "see how the adjustment's going."

"That's just it. I adjusted fine, then everything changed and I'm trying to adjust to that. I'm not ready to adjust to what may or may not happen in the future." My voice goes up a few notches.

"The future is now," he says. It sounds like he's reading something you'd find in a mass-produced fortune cookie. "I have your college prep work sheet right here. The one you were supposed to fill out in English class?"

Ah, yes. The work sheet. I can explain that. But trying to explain it to Mr. Daniel is like playing a guessing game. I want to make him understand, but there are certain words I just can't say.

"Your top three college choices are left blank. Thing is, you had three top college choices when you moved here. Back then you wanted to go to . . . uh . . ." He checks the list. "Scripps College, Pomona College, or Pitzer College. I mean, I've never heard of these schools, but I'm presuming you didn't just make them up. Right?"

Right. "They're legit," I say. "All real, high-quality colleges in the same town: Claremont, California. Where I used to live?"

"Okay, great," Mr. Daniel says. "But they're no longer your top choices because . . . ?"

Because I convinced my boyfriend to go there. Because I don't know why he left so suddenly. Because I don't know why he went without me, and it hurt too much to try to fill out some stupid work sheet. Because maybe the future is now, but that doesn't change the fact that I'm at Haven High and he's at Pitzer College and the space between us is so immense it might as well span several oceans, not a mere 664.08 miles.

It is at that moment the idea comes to me, the way sometimes you come up with the perfect thesis statement for an essay while just standing in the shower. I can fix this. It's so simple.

"You're right," I say, earnest, giving him the eye contact "authority figures" around here really like. "I need to reexamine my priorities. I need to see if the Claremont colleges are still the place for me. I need to make some campus visits."

"Excellent idea," says Mr. Daniel. "Seniors are allowed

three school-excused absences for college visits, you know. Plus, UEA break is coming up." UEA is the Utah name for fall break—and the long weekend is supposedly for educational purposes.

"Looks like I have my work cut out for me, then," I say, standing up. "Thank you for your help, Mr. Daniel."

He beams. "Glad to be of service."

COLLEGE BOUND

Zan and I were going to get out together.

Late last February it was almost warm enough for evening walks, and we would roam the streets of Haven because there was nothing else to do.

"Winter is like this back home, right?" Zan said, almost smiling. "You're used to this kind of cold."

"No, but I like it." I did like it. And it was a cold I wasn't used to, a brisk wind to make your blood curdle but not so much that you had to bundle up. The air smelled like smoke.

"You *like* it?" I could tell from his tone he wasn't talking about the weather.

"I like that you're here," I said. I watched my breath come out in wispy, white bursts, delighting me more than it probably would have on a night that wasn't this night, this night that I was on an evening walk with Alexander Kirchendorf.

Zan stopped walking. He looked at me and smirked.

"You like that I'm here. But what if I weren't here?" We were beneath the industrial glow of a streetlight, and I looked up into his eyes. Was he going to kiss me now?

It hadn't taken me long to learn that kissing at Haven High wasn't like kissing at other schools. Kissing at Haven High was a *big deal*, emphasis added. Victorian-era big deal. I Love You big deal. You saved your kisses for your one and only. Period.

But I was ready for that kiss. I was so ready.

I smiled at him and bit my lower lip lightly, hoping I looked kissable. "You're here right now, aren't you?"

"Someday I won't be."

With Zan, there was so much subtext. He rarely said what he meant, and I loved how figuring him out was like reading *Ulysses*; how understanding one little part made me feel so much smarter. But right now I wanted him to be like a beach read that I could skim and get to the good part. I wanted to get to the hookup.

"Someday I won't be either." I kept my voice light, flirty. "I don't intend to spend the rest of my life here, you know. I'm going back to California soon, for college."

I wasn't sure if I should mention it, but I looked up at him and his eyes were so beautiful and his hair fell so soft against his face and I was reckless with him like I wasn't with anything, or anyone, else. So I said, "Did I ever tell you why I moved here?"

He shook his head.

"My dad's a professor. Philosophy."

"Oh, really?" He said it all blasé, but I could tell he was impressed because his voice got slightly louder and he lifted his head.

"He took a position as a visiting professor here, but he's always taught in Claremont. It's a college town, where I'm from. Not just one college, either. There are five campuses, all running into one another, all distinct but all close to each other. I've wanted to go to Scripps ever since I was a little girl."

"Scripps?" said Zan.

"You should see it. Colleges there look nothing like the ones here." I paused, but it wasn't a long pause because I already knew I was going to say it. "Scripps is a women's college, but it's next to a lot of other good schools. Coed schools."

"Yeah?" Zan was looking at me with this teasing smile, a smile that made me forget how to walk straight. Zan's smiles were so unexpected, such a gift. It was better than a kiss.

Okay, not really. But there was promise in that smile,

and a promise from Alexander Kirchendorf was as good as a kiss.

"I think you'd be a good fit there. At, say, Pitzer." My face said everything my words didn't.

"Pitzer, huh?" Zan raised his eyebrows. "Pitzer College." He smiled at me, the realest, biggest smile I'd ever seen him give anyone. And he'd given it to me.

Me and Pitzer College.

YET ANOTHER TREK OUT
OF THE PARKING LOT

Mattia and I aren't exactly neighbors, but we both live too far from the school to walk, so she drives us to and from school in her piece-of-trash, older-than-I-am white Rabbit, which we refer to as the White Rabbit. Each morning when Mattia picks me up for school, I feel like Alice going to Wonderland.

I meet her out in her B-lot parking space, a coveted spot reserved for students with the seniority and money to get it. "Finally," she says when she sees me. "For a girl who hates Haven High so bad, you certainly take your time getting out of it." She slides into the car and opens my door, which only unlocks from the inside.

"Sorry, I had a meeting." I toss my backpack into the backseat. There's no room for it up front.

"Meeting?" Mattia's puzzled, but not for long. "Did Noah catch up with you?"

"Let me guess. He was looking for me at lunch, and you told him I was in the library."

This is so Mattia: doing what she thinks is best for everyone, even when it isn't. It's the therapist in her, all *communicate, communicate, communicate!* "I had to, Joy. It was just getting too pathetic. So, what happened? Is Zan coming back?"

"He's not coming back."

"Okay." Mattia sounds relieved. Like most people, she doesn't like Zan. Unlike those people, she makes no effort to hide it. She wedges the Rabbit between two Toyotas. There's already a megaline to get out of here. "So what did he want? A guy like Noah Talbot doesn't stalk someone for no reason."

Nobody stalks someone for no reason, but I know what Mattia means. Noah's a Soccer Lovin' Kid, and Soccer Lovin' Kids don't need to go around begging for friends. They automatically have the friendship of everybody in school, if they want it.

Almost everybody, that is. I want nothing to do with the Soccer Lovin' Kids, especially this one. Still, the whole thing's so unlikely I can't help but blow Mattia's mind a little bit. "Oh, it was nothing much, really. He just wants to be my new best friend."

"Whoa, hold up." She brakes too hard for a kid darting across the street. Gotta be a sophomore. "New best friend? For real?" She looks at me, and I know she's picturing me and Noah, BFFs, texting about weekend plans.

I know she's picturing me happy again. The girl doesn't get it.

"Yep. Get this. Before Zan left, he gave Noah specific instructions to pal around with me from time to time."

Her face goes immediately dark. Noah and I will not be BFFs. Noah is obligated to be my pity friend, and it is Zan's fault. Even when he is gone, Zan has messed up. She sighs. "Jeez, that's so tacky and weird. It's like some cowboy in an old Western asking the sheriff to take care of his missus while he's off having some grand adventure. Zan sucks. Seriously. He just sucks."

Why isn't this line moving? Some moron is probably trying to make a left-hand turn. I gaze out the window. Haven High, Home of the Huskies, looks like a prison. There are so few windows it doesn't matter there aren't any bars. The school must have been built back when people thought prisons were attractive, like maybe during the Reagan administration.

"Non sequitur." Ever since Mattia learned about non sequiturs in English, she's been using the term every chance she gets. "About Homecoming."

Great. This routine again. "What about it?"

"You should go." I still haven't figured out why Mattia cares so much about my social life. I spend time with her. Isn't that enough?

"No one's asked me."

"No one's asked you because they know you're still hung up on Zan."

"I'm not 'hung up on Zan.' He's my boyfriend."

"He *was* your boyfriend. Big difference."

"We never broke up," I say, miserable.

Mattia sighs. "Listen, all I know is what you told me. And what you told me is that the night before he left, Zan told you he 'had to get away from this. *All* of this.'" Mattia loves making air quotes. I guess she thinks they make her look more intellectual, but she always bends her fingers so many times it ends up looking like a failed dance move. "Joy, you were part of the all."

I lean my head against the window. Nobody understands. It doesn't matter whether or not I'm part of the "all." The point is I'm not part of the "this." "This" is Noah and his merry band of Soccer Lovin' Kids. "This" is every female crafting on Super-Saturday. "This" is überconservative nutjobs. I am not part of the "this."

"Alexander Kirchendorf is the world's biggest cliché," says Mattia. "He goes off to college, breaking all his high school ties in the process. He reinvents himself as some hotshot linguistics-loving atheist. He'll end up a washed-up has-been, and he'll beg for you back. You better not take him back when he comes crawling, Joy. I'm warning you: I will kick your butt if you do that."

"He always loved linguistics," I mumble. "He didn't just invent that."

I don't want to point out the obvious: if Zan is the world's biggest cliché, then Mattia is Haven's biggest cliché. She's smart but not too smart, peppy but not too peppy, pretty but not too pretty. She'll go to Brigham Young University like forty percent of our class, she'll major in psychology (a subject she's been obsessed with as long as I've known her), and she'll meet the perfect recently returned missionary. They'll get married, have 3.5 children, and get family pictures taken up in the canyon every autumn. It's so easy for people like her.

"You are *way* too good for him," says Mattia, saying what she's supposed to say. "The sooner you move on and see how you deserve to be treated, the better." Realizing we're stuck here a while, she slides the car into park and takes her foot off the brake. "So, about Homecoming. You should go."

This conversation has never actually been a conversation, and only now do I realize I have just as much right to push an agenda as she does. "Hey, did you know we get three school-excused absences to check out institutions of higher learning? What do you say to a college visit? We could road-trip it to Claremont. I could even show you my old house."

"Whoa, non sequitur." She adjusts her sunglasses and

says, "I'm not going to spend three days away from school just to visit some college I'll never go to. I'll miss too much." When Mattia talks about "missing too much" in regards to school, she is not talking about falling behind academically.

"Well, what about next weekend? It's UEA break, so we won't miss any school and—"

"Joy." Mattia rubs her temples. "You're giving me a headache. Besides, I already know where I'm going to school next year."

I know it, too. She's not the right person to go on this trip with me. She can't help me find the part of me that's missing. She's already whole.

There's this long, awkward pause as we inch up to the stop sign.

"So, what, are you going all Zan on me? Leaving town, leaving the Church, leaving everything?"

It's like she's forgotten that I lived in California for sixteen years and in Utah for less than one. "Leaving Haven isn't the same as leaving the Church, you know. They aren't one and the same." What does she think, that if I don't go with her to BYU I'll somehow lose my religion in the process?

"I know, I know." Mattia sighs. "Non sequitur. Are you at least going to the Homecoming game tonight?"

"I already talked to Charlotte about it. If I don't come

to the postgame party at her house, she'll never forgive me. So count me in." Charlotte's the current New Girl— her parents divorced right before senior year. Bad news all around. Now, not only were her parents split up, but she had to spend her last year of high school in a new town. And even worse, that new town was Haven.

I was the first person to talk to her. When we picked lab partners in AP bio I looked around the class and— surprise—didn't see anyone I knew. But I knew the look on Charlotte's face. It was bafflement mixed with ter- ror—classic *where-am-I-and-when-can-I-get-out?* I asked her if she wanted to partner up, told her I was a trans- plant to this school, too. A connection like that can make you friends for life. It's the New Girl code.

Mattia smiles and I know I'm slowly winning her back. "There's no way you'd bother with the game if Zan was around," she says. "Maybe his leaving is a good thing."

The girl never knows when to quit. "So, about the col- lege visit," I mimic her perfectly. "You should go."

POTENTIAL ROAD TRIP CANDIDATES

~~Mattia~~

Charlotte

Kristine

? ? ?

SECRET LIFE OF A GOLDEN BOY

I hate football. I never used to go to games at my old high school because, as I told Gretel, "our high school football games are the biggest waste of time ever."

I was so wrong.

Haven High School football games may well be the most pointless events on the planet. Everybody knows who's going to win before the games even start—the Huskies haven't won a game in seven seasons. The only good thing about this is that I can show up to the game at halftime, knowing I haven't missed anything.

I flash my student ID at the gate and wander through the maze that is the concession area. It seems like every club at school is trying to get rich off of the fact that there's nothing to do at sporting events except eat. I head for the bleachers, detouring past a line of people who want to buy pretzels from the marching band.

"Joy!" I was hoping to hear someone call my name, but not this someone.

A bunch of blond groupies scatter from Noah's wake

as he walks toward me, smiling. I know he wants to "be a friend," but this run-in just seems forced and awkward.

"Hey, what have you got there?" He's holding a huge box, cryptically labeled $1.00.

"Caramel apple pops. Want one? It's for a good cause."

"What cause?" I don't mean for it to come out sounding suspicious. If Noah Talbot says it's for a good cause, who am I to doubt?

"Girls' basketball team." He hands me a sucker.

"Why are you selling candy for the girls' team?"

"Equipment manager."

"Oh," I say, wondering why anyone would choose to be an equipment manager, least of all admit to it so readily. Especially a Soccer Lovin' Kid—in the Haven world, playing varsity soccer is about a thousand times more prestigious than playing basketball. Soccer is our thing. Other sports . . . well, aren't. "I'd love to support the team, but I don't have any money left. Spent it all on a ticket." I hand the candy back to him.

He waves it away. "Consider it a gift."

"Joy!" This time it really is Mattia, calling to me from high in the bleachers, even though she knows I hate heights. This kind of thing is her idea of helping me "conquer my phobias." What a pal.

"I have to go. Thanks for the caramel apple pop,

though. I'll be sure to recommend them to my friends." I purposely don't look at him as I walk away.

"See you tonight at Charlotte's?" he calls out.

I breathe in deep. "Maybe." I don't want to go to Charlotte's. I don't want to celebrate Homecoming like it's New Year's Eve. I hate this year. I don't want to live this year. I want Zan.

After climbing over the legs of about a bazillion people, I reach my friends.

"Where'd you get that?" Kristine points to my sucker.

"Nowhere," I say, and shove it into my jacket pocket. "What's the score?"

JUST TO RECAP: WHY I CAN'T
BE FRIENDS WITH NOAH

1. He's a Soccer Lovin' Kid and enjoys such lame frivolity as Beverage Night.

2. He's a Soccer Lovin' Kid and thus a popular kid. I don't hang out with popular kids.

3. He's a Soccer Lovin' Kid. They're the ones who made Zan leave.

WHY I'M LATE TO CHARLOTTE'S

I don't want anyone to know I'm looking for Zan. It would seem obsessive. Give him his space, they'd say. He didn't give you his new address for a reason. He changed his phone number for a reason. Stalking people is just wrong.

I checked the student directory on the Pitzer website at the beginning of the year. They had Zan on record, but none of his information was available. I figured they hadn't added details about new students yet.

I've checked every day since. I've bookmarked the page.

Zan doesn't want anyone to find him, I know that.

But I can't believe it.

A WORD-OF-MOUTH PARTY

Charlotte lives in a normal-size house on a lot that measures the length of a football field from the front porch to the back fence. It's the house her dad grew up in, the house where her grandparents still live, the house where Charlotte and her father have returned.

In preparation for the party, she's strung Japanese lanterns from the trees, and in the twilight they illuminate the stream running through the backyard. I've got to hand it to her—the place looks magical. Now I can see her starting a bonfire in the pit, bags of marshmallows and packages of Hershey bars at her side. Perfect. I'll go help her. I will not think of Zan.

The problem is Alyssa. I've purposely come solo to the party, and purposely late, too, hoping to sneak in and avoid talking to any and all people outside of my circle. Alyssa's so far outside my circle I'm surprised we're even at the same party. Although I'm sure this is exactly what Charlotte wanted, as the New Girl in school: a party with guests she doesn't even know, a word-of-mouth party.

That was me, once. That was what I'd wanted. I'd wanted Zan. But I'd wanted friends, too.

Now I know all these kids well enough to know I want nothing to do with any of them. I know that Alyssa's been the official school gossip since they all went to Haven School for Tots, or whatever fine establishment it was that turned my classmates into my classmates.

Alyssa walks over. She's short and slender, but she towers over me in her see-through wedge sandals. In addition to school gossip, she's also known as school skank, which at Haven High means that the pink cami under her hoodie shows the slightest hint of cleavage. "I've heard Zan's in California."

"Yeah," I say, noncommittal, when it's clear she's waiting for a response. "He went to college. Some people do that, you know—go to school somewhere out of state."

"Well, I heard he was selling pot. And carving driftwood on the beach?" She looks up at me, her wide blue eyes framed by lashes coated in blue mascara.

Pot? Driftwood? Please. She doesn't know Zan, and this makes it even more obvious. Nobody in this town knows Zan. Nobody in this town cares about Zan. As far as gossip goes, this is B-list, at best. Zan is only A-list to me.

I want to look around for Mattia, but Alyssa's managed to rope me into a power-stare. If I look away I'll be admitting defeat, and even though this game is stupid, it's crucial that I win.

"I wanted to confirm with you before I told anyone else." Her voice holds a challenge, but I don't know what it is.

"Very generous of you," I say evenly. That's all the skank's getting.

Mattia's picked up on the help-me vibes I've been sending and she's talking before she even reaches me. "There you are, Joy, I've been looking all over for you!" There's a fake smile to Alyssa, a tug to my arm, and we're off, just like that. "C'mon, I've staked us out a place to sit by the fire." She motions to a bench where Kristine is sitting, talking to some guy reclining on the lowest branch of the cherry tree next to her.

"Alyssa thinks Zan's a drug dealer who carves driftwood on the beach," I tell Mattia, still in a daze.

Mattia rolls her eyes. "Alyssa thinks wearing thongs instead of V-strings make her classy. Forget Alyssa. Come chill."

I take in a long breath through my nose and try to relax, but my body is having none of it.

The fire gets started and real night falls, with darkness and crickets and burned marshmallows and the Haven High spirit song sung by two dozen seniors who have prepared themselves for this moment their whole lives.

I watch Noah in sideways glimpses. Never long enough that he can feel it. Just hummingbird-fast glances.

Sometimes I envy him. Noah looks so happy, pounding it hello to the other guys, smiling at the girls in his casual, nonthreatening way of flirting. The girls know there's no possibility with him, which of course makes them like him even more.

None of the male Soccer Lovin' Kids have girlfriends. They'll all go on two-year missions after graduation, and they don't want to get serious with a girl before they leave. Mattia told me this when I first moved in and was trying to figure out who was coupled up.

"It's to keep people from getting hurt," she explained. "That way they don't have to break up when he leaves. Or if they don't break up, she doesn't have to spend two years pining away for him while he's gone."

It all sounded very practical, but totally foreign. How is it that easy? How do you decide not to fall in love and then keep yourself from doing it? It didn't make any sense.

But right now, it does. Noah does not look like a guy who, less than two months ago, lost his best friend. Noah has lots of guys to fill that void. It's probably the same way with girls. He doesn't need a girlfriend because there's always someone there to flirt with or take to a dance or hang out with at a party. It's all so easy for him.

It's who he is. He doesn't have to hurt.

Eventually the fire gets low and so does the crowd. Alyssa waves bye like we're tight now. I resist giving her the finger. A half-eaten marshmallow sits dejectedly on a patch of flattened grass. Show's over. Mattia, Kristine, and I are staying over for one of our customary Friday-night sleepovers.

"We're going inside to get our stuff," says Mattia. "You coming?"

"In a minute." There's something soothing in staying just where I am, alone for a little while. I shiver. It's too cold to be sleeping outside, but we are young and adventurous, ready for anything. But that part of me is gone. It left when Zan did.

He should be here. His arm should be around me and I should be snuggling close, staying warm. He should be reminding me how much he loves my vanilla perfume, how lucky he is to be here with me, how much he wishes he could sleep over, too. I should be punching him playfully right now, rolling my eyes, saying "You're such a *guy*—you only want one thing!"

Except Zan didn't want one thing. He wanted everything.

When I finally go inside to brush my teeth, I look through the glazed glass of the bathroom window. I can hear Mattia's loud, almost-obnoxious laugh, and the chain reaction of Kristine's giggles. It all feels like another world. I grab my sleeping bag from Charlotte's bedroom and head outside.

They have already laid their sleeping bags out like the spokes of a bicycle wheel. I set my bag where the last spoke should be, an empty space next to Mattia. She is talking, her tone wistful, the effect enhanced by the Japanese lantern casting a slanted glow on her face. "It was over by the late eighties, really."

"So sad," Kristine says. "Such a waste. Our generation never had a chance."

"What about . . . you know . . . a reemergence?" Charlotte sounds hopeful.

I snuggle into my sleeping bag. "What's the topic of discussion?"

"The gradual demise of Spin the Bottle," says Mattia.

The demise of Spin the Bottle? "Even when it was in existence, I don't think Spin the Bottle was exactly popular with the seventeen-year-old set," I say.

Everybody stares at me.

"I mean, I hate to be the voice of reason here, but . . ." I shrug.

"I think it had to do with the disappearance of bottles," says Kristine. "When everybody started drinking soda from a can, *that's* when it tapered off."

"Non sequitur," says Mattia. "Which guys got smoking hot over the summer?"

"Sorry, I don't know anything, but who was that guy in the blue polo shirt with the matching eyes that spent most of the night on the rope swing?" About two-thirds of Charlotte's questions start out with apologies.

"His two eyes matched each other?" I say. "Sounds like a real catch." I'm half dreading half hoping she's talking about who I think she's talking about.

"Eyes that matched his shirt!" Charlotte throws her teddy bear and it hits me dead-on. It stings more than I expect, due to its beanbaggy backside.

"Blond hair and a tendency toward whistling?" Kristine can identify anyone in the senior class by mannerisms that the average observer doesn't even pick up on.

"Yeah, that's him. He's way good looking. We should hang out with him sometime." Charlotte doesn't dare meet new people without our permission and promise we will be there, too. Whether she is shy or just unsure of the social strata, Mattia says Charlotte is dependent to an extreme.

"I don't know," says Kristine. "Your whistling fool is Noah Talbot, and he's not Joy's bestest bud at the moment."

"Actually, he is," I say, pulling my sleeping bag up to cover my arms. "Or at least he wants to be. He thinks we should be 'friends.'" I air quote the word like Mattia does to show the impossibility of it.

"Noah Talbot." Charlotte pauses. "*He's* the guy who's stalking Joy?"

"What, I don't deserve a good-looking stalker?" I say, joking, and then curse myself for admitting I think he's good looking.

Charlotte's too preoccupied thinking she's offended me to notice.

"I'm just kidding, Char. But trust me—you don't want to hang out with Noah Talbot. Even Zan doesn't want to hang out with Noah Talbot, and they're best friends."

"*Were* best friends," Mattia corrects. "Now Noah wants to be best friends with you instead."

"No, no—*he* doesn't want to be friends with me. He thinks Zan wants him to be friends with me. But Zan just wants . . ." What does Zan want? "Zan just wants to be left alone by the Noahs of the world."

HOW I MET NOAH

My seventeenth birthday fell six weeks after I moved to Haven.

Frankly, I hadn't even planned to have a birthday party. Before the move, I was hoping my parents would fly me back to California. Home to see Gretel, home to see everything I'd left behind.

Six weeks was long enough for my entire world to change. Six weeks was long enough for me to start at a school where the lyrics to the school song sounded suspiciously similar to a Mormon hymn. Six weeks was long enough to become best friends with an outgoing Husky Ambassador and have people to sit with at lunch every day. Six weeks was long enough for me to fall for a boy with a brilliant mind and secondhand shoes. But, according to my parents, six weeks was not long enough to merit a trip back to California.

I was okay with that—really. It gave me a chance to have a party and invite Zan. We could hang out together like a real couple. It would solidify us: ZanandJoy. JoyandZan.

Mattia loved the idea and invited everyone she knew. "This is such a great way for you to fully adapt to your new environment!" she squealed, like the psychology-major-in-training she was. She'd already set up a Facebook page to track the party details by the time I thought to double-check with Zan.

"Next Friday?" Zan said when I told him. He furrowed his brow, concerned. "I have class Friday, remember?"

Zan was technically a junior at the same university where my dad taught, as well as a junior at Haven High, so between the two schools he practically always had class. "Yeah, but class only goes until six, right? Plenty of time for you to get back and freshen up." I smiled at him. "And wrap my birthday present, of course."

"Of course," said Zan. "Except that this is the last class before midterms and some of us are having a study group after. It could go pretty late."

"You don't need a study group—you're way smarter than anybody else in that class. You just don't want to go to a Haven party," I teased. Six weeks was long enough that I'd already experienced Haven parties, where activities often included Disney movies. Refreshments consisted of two liters of Sprite and peanut-butter cookies with Hershey's Kisses on top.

"Well," he said, "I *don't* want to go to a Haven party." He gave his signature almost-smile, eyebrows raised. "But I would, for you. I wouldn't even bother with the study group in the first place, except this prof has a weird testing-style. I really need to do this."

"I understand," I said. And being familiar with the world of academia, I did. Not that I wasn't disappointed. It hurt like losing a contest you had no real intention of winning. You expect to lose, but there's still that sinking-in-the-chest when you find out.

I wanted him to be there, but the rules of life dictated otherwise. I needed him to know I understood that. I wasn't some ditzy Haven girl who didn't get it. "I'll save you a cookie," I told him.

I never thought the party would become what it did—a word-of-mouth party—and I was surprised at how happy it made me to fit so well inside this strange, small new world. I could have Zan. I could also have a party where a girl I didn't know was on the karaoke machine in the family room, belting out some song I'd never heard.

A happy medium—that was the best birthday present I could have gotten. Zan and I could mock Haven all we wanted in our own private moments. We could plan our escape. But I could still have friends, too.

People were playing board games in the living room—Twister, Cranium, Taboo. I was in the kitchen, refilling a bowl of tortilla chips. Mattia and Kristine were at the dining-room table with a few guys, playing a card game involving spoons.

"Happy birthday."

I stopped pouring, turned around, and there was Noah Talbot.

"Thanks." I don't know why I was surprised to see him. It was a word-of-mouth party, after all, and besides, he was Zan's best friend. I mean, as much as a guy like Zan, who prided himself on being too good for Havenites, could actually have a Havenite best friend.

"Here," Noah said too quickly, shoving something at me. "This is from Zan."

I just stared at him. True, he was Zan's "best friend," but I hardly knew Noah Talbot. He and Zan lived next door to each other—had forever—which is why they were friends. Proximity. Other than that, they had nothing in common.

I shifted the package from one hand to the other. From the size and shape, I could tell it was a book. "Oh. Well . . . thanks for bringing it for him."

Noah licked his upper lip. It was subtle, but he looked anxious to leave. He probably hadn't even wanted to be here. No other Soccer Lovin' Kids were at the party, as far as I knew.

I was sure Noah was going to leave, but instead he said, "Joy, I know you don't like me."

And it was true. I *didn't* like him. But it wasn't an active kind of dislike. He was a popular kid, and I didn't feel comfortable around the popular kids.

It was more than that, though. I didn't like any of the Soccer Lovin' Kids, just by essence of them being Soccer Lovin' Kids. I didn't like how easy it was for all of them, how they all *were* Haven. They knew the sport they were supposed to play, so they did. They knew what they were supposed to look like, so they did. They knew what they were supposed to believe, so they did. But none of them were real to me. Noah wasn't real to me.

"I don't really know you," is what I said.

"We'll have to change that," he said, smiling at me. It was a Haven smile: white, straight teeth, dimples, eye contact. Friendly, yet completely hollow.

"Sure, yeah," I said. But it's like in the summer when you run into someone from school and say, "Let's hang out sometime." It's just what you say—no one has any intention of really acting on it.

"Joy." He reached out and shook my hand, which was

72

weird, even for him. "I hope you have a really great birthday. And I hope this is a really great year."

"Um . . . thanks." I tried to smile. "You're welcome to stay and hang out, have something to drink." There was a big tub of ice next to me, filled with soda. It was mostly Sprite and I half smiled, thinking of how much Zan would hate this if he were here.

Noah grabbed a can. "I'll see you around," he said, shaking off the melted ice before he turned to leave.

"See ya," I said. "Let's hang out sometime."

DREAM SEQUENCE

I believe that a person should try to understand dreams and take warning from them, which is why I keep coming up crazy on these psychological "personality inventories" Mattia's always making me take online. Supposedly, these tests are designed to tell you who's certifiable and who isn't.

I am.

I've dreamed of Zan each night since he's left. He's got a hold on me harder now than he did when we were together.

I dream Zan is in the school, staring into the cheap vending machine, deciding on his sugar-snack of choice. I am on the other side of the school, running to him, hoping to get there before he can make the wrong selection. By the time I reach him, panting, it's too late. He's chomping on a Reese's cup, convincing me not to worry.

Of course I do anyway. I know Zan so well he's an extension of me. His needs are my needs. I know the truth about him.

He's allergic to peanuts.

I wake—cold above me, cold below me, face wet from tears or dew or sweat. Around me there's no sound but sleeping, no smell but outside. Go back to sleep.

I don't sleep. Every shadow I see is Zan. The hand I warm with my hand is Zan's, even if it is connected to my body.

A person should try to understand dreams. A person should take warning from them.

AND THE COLD HARD TRUTH IS

I'm going to Claremont with Noah.
I saw it in a dream.
I don't want to believe it.
But that's what the dream said to do.

HOMECOMING

On Saturday night my parents have a reservation at Bonjourno, the only nice restaurant in Haven, and I have a reservation with my biology textbook. Bonjourno will no doubt be packed with Homecoming couples tonight, and I hope it won't make Mom and Dad feel sorry for me when they realize I'm not one of them.

"Have a good time," I tell them, piling various school supplies on the kitchen table. This is how I love to study— plenty of space, my pink highlighter, and a pineapple– green pepper pizza from Papa John's on the way. It makes it okay that I'm studying biology, my nemesis.

"Be good," my mother says. I can tell she feels obligated to say something motherly, but I bet she's thinking, *Have fun with your cations and lipids!*

It truly makes me feel pathetic. But I remember the pizza and the feeling passes.

If you follow the "college track" at Haven High then you take AP biology as a senior, but Zan did things his own way and took microbiology at the community college last year. If only I had taken that as a warning. If only I had realized how badly he wanted to leave. If only I had seen how much he wanted to change himself. If only I had listened when he went on and on about the wonders of mitosis.

I hear a knock: three short, three long, then three more short. Finally. Nourishment. There's pizza money on the counter, so I grab it and open the door.

It's not pizza.

On my doorstep, dressed in a dark, oversize suit and holding out a red rose, is Noah Talbot.

MY JOY

The first time I knew I was really, truly, from-the-depths-of-my-soul in love with Alexander Kirchendorf was the night of our first kiss—the night he called me His Joy.

Prom night and we were rocking on the old-fashioned porch swing outside my house. We had been discussing something, I don't remember what, when we both stopped talking and stopped listening. I remember thinking: *he is going to kiss you now, move in closer, move*—but being frozen with fright and delight. We both sat there, suspended in something much thicker than silence, for what seemed like a thousand hours. He touched my face, my lips. He whispered to me: "My Joy." And maybe it wasn't perfect, but it was good enough for me, and when I let him kiss me I knew that this was the man I wanted to spend eternity with.

HOMECOMING, PART II

"Noah?" Did my dream last night will him to be here, on my doorstep?

No, that's too absurd a thought even for me to believe. Then why is he here?

He steps forward. "Will you go to Homecoming with me?" He hands me the rose.

"Why? What happened to your date?" Showing up at a girl's door at eight o'clock and asking her to go to the dance with you is not how traditional dating is done in Haven.

Haven dating follows a different set of rules. Here is what should have happened: About three weeks ago, Noah should have decided on a happy, nondescript blonde to take to the dance. He should have gotten a jigsaw puzzle, written his name on the back, and distributed the pieces in a box of Kix cereal. After writing a poem to the effect of "I get a KIX out of you. Will you go to Homecoming with me?" he should have dropped the box on her doorstep. She would have replied in an equally clever way. He should have picked her up early in the day and taken her to do something like play three-legged football or go on a scavenger hunt for the needy with the other twelve couples in their group. Then he should have taken her home, picked up her corsage, and gotten into his suit, prepared to take her out to dinner someplace nice.

Bonjourno. He should be at Bonjourno right now, telling some girl I don't know, or care to know, that her dress looks pretty. He should not be here, dressed up, asking a girl in gray sweats with a highlighter in her hair for a date.

"I don't have a date. I'm hoping you'll help me remedy that problem." Noah looks so cute standing there, smiling. He doesn't look at all self-conscious, just happy, just wondering. "Can I come in?"

"I guess." I open the door wider. "I was studying." The only light that's on is in the kitchen, so he starts walking in that direction without me saying anything.

He picks the book off the table. "Biology," he says. "How come you're always studying biology when I run into you?"

"Because I'm always studying biology, period. So I don't think I can go to the dance with you. Sorry." I set the rose in my water glass. "Thanks, though."

"What if I help you with biology, then we go?"

"Noah, why don't you just go with someone else? Someone who wants to go?"

"You don't want to go?" Noah asks, his big eyes wide and sad.

It must be the sad eyes that give me the sudden, stupid urge to protect him. "It's not that, it's just . . ." The doorbell rings. "I'll be right back," I say, walking over to the door.

"Is it because you don't have a dress?"

"Somebody here order a pizza?" asks a big dark-haired guy in a red polo shirt.

I nod, ignoring the dress question, which is too ridiculous to answer anyway.

"Is that your car?" The pizza guy isn't looking at me, which is maybe an insult, but I don't care. Noah nods, and the guy whistles. "Sweet ride."

I glance over the pizza guy's shoulder. One of the two cars in my driveway has a neon pizza slice on the roof. The other one doesn't look that sweet to me—standard Haven High "old car." The outside lights aren't bright, and I'm not a car person, but still. I can see what's right in front of me: a boxy sky blue hatchback with black trim. Impressive it is not.

"Thank you, sir," Noah says, and I look at him, all earnest-faced and cleanly shaven. "So what's the deal, Joy? Are you embarrassed to be seen with me?"

"Does it have a turbo?" The pizza guy interrupts. I have no idea what he's talking about, but apparently the comment's again directed at Noah. Noah nods, and the guy does, too, before whistling again. I hate whistling. I just want everybody out of my house so I can study without talking about turbos and Homecoming dresses.

"That car's nothing to be ashamed of," the pizza guy says, staring like he expects better from me. "You girls don't understand the difference between old and vintage. That baby out there, that's a SAAB nine hundred. A classic. I know collectors who would *kill* for that puppy." I'm sick of being harassed by this guy, and I want my food. Plus I'm disturbed by the many terms of endearment he uses for an inanimate object. But before I can say anything he finishes his thought with, "That'll be thirteen seventy-three."

I shove fifteen dollars onto the pizza box, giving him a minitip because of my extreme dissatisfaction with his service. He scoops up the money, handing me the box.

To complete my humiliation in front of this delivery guy I don't even like, Noah adds one last zinger. "Is this because you're still too in love with Zan to consider going anywhere with someone else?"

The pizza man's eyebrows go up, and I slam the door. "It isn't that, Noah. I just don't really like dances. And I have this pizza here, and the whole house to myself, and I need to study."

"You don't really like dances?"

I shake my head. "Not really. I don't like dancing."

Zan and I went to one dance. Other dances I could totally do without, and I could have done without this one, too, but part of me said prom was a must-do, at least once. So we said hi to my friends, danced one song at my request, and left. There was no elaborate day activity, no big group, no standing in long lines for pictures against cheesy backdrops. I didn't like dances. Neither did he. We preferred each other to sweaty bodies and obnoxious DJs.

Noah loosens his burgundy tie. "Good. I don't like dancing, either." He eyes the pizza. "So, what kind did you order?"

"Pineapple and green pepper." I can't help being embarrassed. I wish I had ordered something normal people like. Why? He's the one who showed up here uninvited. Still, the hostess in me says, "Would you like a slice?"

"Love one. I'm starved." He takes off his jacket and hangs it across the dining-room chair. He plans to stay.

"You don't mind pineapple with green peppers?" Most people do. Zan did.

"Nope. I like it. I'm a vegetarian." He starts opening random cupboards. "Where do you keep plates?"

"You're a vegetarian?" Vegetarian seems way too off-the-beaten-path for someone like him. I grab two paper plates from a lower shelf. "I didn't know that."

"How would you? You don't know me very well yet, do you?"

"No," I say. "Not yet." *Not ever,* is what I think. Or, rather, what I want to think. Because the first thing I actually think is, *Why?* I must also say it out loud, because Noah looks up from his pizza, surprised.

"Why don't you know me?"

"No, why are you vegetarian?"

He shrugs. "Animals are friends—not food."

"You're an animal lover? Seriously?" I grin. Noah Talbot, friend to animals . . . "Let me guess, you've wanted to build your own ark ever since you learned about the guy you were named after."

"Hey, my man Noah was a wicked awesome prophet. You have a problem with that?"

I just shake my head and walk to the fridge.

"This is fun," Noah says. He pops a crescent moon of crust into his mouth and swallows. "You know, hanging out. Why didn't we do this sooner?"

He's the one who invited himself over here. He's eating *my* pizza, crust first into his big mouth, with his jacket (and, now that I notice it, his tie) draped over *my* chair. And he's all, "Wow, why didn't I mooch off you sooner?"

Must be nice in Land of the Popular, where you can just assume everyone wants your company. "You know why."

"No I don't." When I look at him it's clear that he doesn't.

"You made my boyfriend leave. You were all, 'Hi, I'm Everything Stupid About Haven.'" Since my original water glass is now being used as a vase, I pour a second. It leaves the pitcher nearly empty.

Noah rolls his eyes, but to his credit, he doesn't try to change my mind. "Why didn't we hang out before Zan left, then? Before I apparently pushed him over the edge because I'm all that is wrong with the world?"

"Not all that's wrong with *the* world. All that's wrong with *this* world." I can't figure out if he understands the difference. "You want something to drink?"

His face lights up. "Do you have Sprite?"

Sprite. It's such a Noah drink. I check the fridge door and find a can hidden behind a bottle of ketchup. I have no idea how old either of them are, but I've always considered food in the fridge door to have an indefinite shelf life.

"Noah," I ask, setting down my water glass and handing him the soda, "why are you here? You should be at the dance right now, getting crowned Homecoming King or whatever it is people like you do."

He tips onto the back legs of his kitchen chair. I hate

it when people do that. I'm petrified they're going to fall. "People like me," he says, "get crowned Homecoming King at the *game.*"

"Oh, sorry," I say, not sorry at all. "All four on the floor, right now." I point at his chair. "House rule."

"Oh, sorry," he says, not sorry at all. He tilts his chair back to normal and looks at me. "And I'm not Homecoming King." He looks sheepish. "I'm on the Homecoming Court."

"Whatever." I can feel Noah looking at me. I can't meet his gaze.

"Yeah, that's how I felt, too. Whatever. I just wasn't in the mood to go out in the same group like everything is the same. It isn't. Zan is gone."

"Why do you care if Zan's gone?" Now I do look at him, because what right does he have to get all weepy about this? It's not the same for him as it is for me. "You have a ton of other friends."

Noah looks surprised, then his eyes get serious. "Just because I have lots of friends doesn't mean I care about each one of them less."

Wow. Didn't see that coming.

And there's no denying it: I'm humiliated. Like honestly humiliated. Because Mr. Haven High Homecoming Court, who doesn't need a girlfriend or even a best friend for that matter, might actually have some depth after all.

And he knows. He definitely knows, because my face has gone red or pale or blank or whatever it's done. He knows what I'm feeling. So he does something far more gracious than anything I've done tonight: he changes the subject.

THE ART OF HOMEMAKING

"So what gives with the books?" Noah says. "I've been wondering all night." He tips back on his chair for a second, but only a second, before remembering.

I forgot about the books. I always forget about the books when someone new comes over because to me, the books have always been there, as much a part of the house as the sofa or the knife block. We have books on shelves, of course: our kitchen flows into our dining room which flows into our family room and every available inch of wall space has bookcases. But we also have books in stacks. Well, not just books—old periodicals, too. It's like we have a dozen almost-finished games of Jenga on our floor.

"It's my mom's job," I say, relieved to be talking about someone other than Noah or Zan. "She sells books."

With his mouth, Noah says, "Oh, cool." But with every other part of his body, Noah says that this space looks less like a Barnes & Noble and more like a garage that needs to be cleaned.

"It's an eBay store," I explain, before biting into my pizza. "Someone's in the Kitchen with Diana. She sells vintage cookbooks, like the 1952 edition of Betty Crocker. And other stuff that's hard to find."

"Oh, cool," says Noah, and this time I know he really means it. He picks up a copy of a World War II–era cooking magazine in not-bad condition. "So how does your mom manage to find these?"

"Thrift shops, garage sales, used-book stores, the usual suspects. She has an eye for the good stuff." As I'm saying it, I already know this puts an end to the conversation. What is there to say after that?

Since I'm expecting the silence, the pause seems much longer than it really is. Noah flips through *Fun Theme Parties* circa 1967 and I consider grabbing another slice of pizza, just to have something to chew on, just to have something to do besides look up or look down. Something to do besides think about the person I'm really thinking about. The person I'm going to be thinking about for the rest of my life.

"I don't know why I'm telling you all this," I say, finally.

"I do," he says. "It's because you don't want to talk to me about Zan."

I laugh, but it's a miserable laugh. "If I talk to you about Zan, I'll never stop."

ZAN

I want to hold on to Zan the way a junkie resists rehab, or a dieter rationalizes a chocolate éclair; the way forbidden lovers run from inevitable consequence. The instant gratification of one last time makes me shake with satisfaction. But when his memory is gone I feel the aching return like a bruise that won't heal.

HOME LEAVING

"I can't talk about him to anyone else." It's just occurred to me that although Noah will never be a friend, maybe in some ways he's better than a friend. "My friends won't even let me mention him. To them, he's just some ex-boyfriend that we're never to speak of again." I start tapping my pink highlighter against my biology book. Do I say it? Do I want to? Do I dare?

"I miss him, too," Noah says.

That's all I need. "Then let's go find him!"

"What do you mean?" *Fun Theme Parties* is open to a picture of a football cake, with green glass bowls of M&M's next to it. "We already know where he is. His parents already know where he is. He doesn't need to be found."

"He doesn't *want* to be found. There's a difference."

Noah looks at me, confused, before turning back to his book. "If he doesn't want to be found, than why would we want to go find him? He obviously doesn't want to see us. Or anyone from his 'deep, dark past.'"

"We are not part of his past! All he needs to do is see us and he'll remember that!" I start in on my Mattia spiel. "Listen, we get three school-excused absences to check out colleges. Besides, UEA break is next week anyway. We can take your car! You know, since it's vintage and all. I totally want to road trip in that!" That part, of course, isn't the truth. But since it's something I *wish* was the truth, I don't think it qualifies as a lie. "We can go to Claremont, stay with my friends there, and find out where Zan—"

"Joy," he says. "Zan doesn't want to be found."

"Maybe not. But I need closure."

I think of Noah's serious eyes when he said, "Just because I have a lot of friends doesn't mean I care about each one of them any less." I know he understands even before I ask him if he does.

I can't read his expression.

"I'm going with or without you," I say. But I'm not going without him. I know it even before he sighs and nods his head.

"You're crazy, you know that? It's like you go out looking for ways to get hurt."

Does Noah look disappointed? Even if he does, I don't care.

I'm going to Claremont with Noah. I saw it in a dream.

NINETY-SIX PERCENT NEUROTIC

As hard as I try, I'll never be as cool as Gretel Addison. She's witty, sophisticated, and just counterculture enough to remain someone I aspire to be, but will never reach.

Gretel is the type who gives henna tattoos, burns patchouli incense, and drinks all-natural soda. She'll put purple streaks in her hair just for fun. When we were little, we'd always come up with stupid get-rich-quick schemes. We sold lemonade, snickerdoodles, and fudge that was always burned. Once we even made perfume, throwing in tea bags and vanilla extract. Now jasmine is her signature scent.

We take advantage of our free weekend minutes every Sunday night, but this Sunday night is different. This Sunday night I tell her: "I'm coming to Claremont, and I need a place to crash."

"Yeah, of course," she says. Gretel's quick to process— I love that about her. "Now give me the details—in descending order of importance."

"First detail," I say, "is that I need closure."

She's quiet for just two seconds too long. "Meaning what, exactly?"

"Meaning that in three days I'll be at Pitzer, finding Zan and getting my life back."

"How is that closure?" She exhales, long and deep, and I know she thinks this is a bad idea but isn't going to say so because she knows it's useless. There's so much comfort in knowing exactly what someone will do, exactly how someone will react, not because you saw it in a dream but because you know them so well. "So, basically you're planning to come here and get him back, right? In fact, don't answer that. I already know I'm right."

"Gretel," I say, tracing the pattern on my bedspread, "I took this personality analysis last week that gave me a score of ninety-six on neuroticism. Do you think it was out of a hundred?"

"Undoubtedly," she says without missing a beat. "So when do you get here?"

MONDAY MORNING: DETAIL #1

Charlotte is my alibi.

"Okay," she says when I ask. No annoying questions. No remarks about Zan. Ditto about Noah. Ditto about the trip. She just says she'll cover for me, say I'm staying with her at her mom's over the break, and we make a plan.

"Your parents won't care if you tell them you're staying with me while I visit my mom for the long weekend," she says. "Trust me. Nothing ever happens in my old neighborhood. It's a parent's dream-come-true vacation destination." She bites her lip, thinking, making sure we have our bases covered. Charlotte is nothing if not thorough. "If your mom or dad calls you, they probably won't want to talk to me, but if they do just tell them I'm in the shower. That always seems to work on TV."

"Thanks, Char."

"You need this, Joy." I know she really gets it. "But why don't you just tell your parents you're going to Claremont with Noah? You know, so you wouldn't have to lie." She's not saying it like a judgment; she's just saying it because she knows that generally I'm in favor of telling the truth. "I mean, aren't you worried they're going to find out? And they seem cool."

And for the most part, they are cool. That's the problem. I like my parents. I care what they think. If I told them I was going to visit colleges, they'd be hurt that I didn't want them to come along. If I told them I was going to find Zan, I don't know if they'd disapprove or not, but I know without a doubt they'd think less of me. I just can't handle that right now. Then, throw Noah into the whole equation and . . . "It's too complicated."

"More complicated than this?" She looks unconvinced.

"Just trust me."

"I do," she says. "That's the problem. I think I might be the only one."

MONDAY NIGHT

I am dreaming. It is that point in a dream when you know it's a dream. You know it's temporary. You know it isn't real. But you still don't wake yourself.

It is lunchtime and Zan and I are outside the Haven High library. There is me; there is Zan; there is silence. A sophomore punk is cursing the stuck Milky Way in the cheap vending machine, and I know I should hear him, but I don't. I only hear Zan. Zan says: "Joy, when did you love me?"

I am swimming in his eyes, in his hot-chocolate eyes. "Now, Zan. I love you now."

Mattia and Charlotte and Kristine walk by, and I know they're laughing, but I can't hear them. They don't see me. They don't see Zan.

"When did you love me?" Zan asks, more urgent this time. "When did you love me?"

I don't want to answer, so I start kissing him instead. I kiss him hard—too hard, maybe. He pushes me away from him, and I stumble backward, into Noah.

"Joy?" Noah says it in a voice much deeper than his regular one. "What's going on? I thought you two had broken up."

Broken up. Broken up. Broken up. The words swirl around my head until they sound foreign. Broken up. Broken up.

The bell rings, and I don't hear it, I feel it. I can't move. Broken up. Broken up. Broken up.

Now the bell is loud enough to hear and I hear it but I still can't move. Broken up. Broken up.

It's not the bell. It's the alarm clock.

Time for school.

THE PLAN

Who: JA, NT
What: College Visit
Code name: Operation Closure
When: Thursday morning through Sunday
night. Conveniently scheduled to
coincide with UEA break.
Days absent from school: 0.
Where: Claremont, CA
How: NT's classic SAAB 900 (JA will
pay her share of the gas $$$)

THIS INFORMATION IS CONFIDENTIAL

TUESDAY AFTERNOON:
DETAIL #2

After school I go to Phil's Market. Slightly dangerous, since approximately eighty-two percent of Haven High's student body works at Phil's.

I purchase Pop-Tarts and trail mix and Chips Ahoy! and granola bars and potato chips and pretzels and cheese and crackers. I buy tiny bottles of orange juice and big bottles of Sprite.

"Having a party?" the checker says, scanning my items. I recognize him from school, think his name is Chris. His name tag reads: I'M JOSE, HOW CAN I HELP YOU?

This roundup of road-trip food would make for a pretty lame party, even by Haven High standards, but I just smile; just keep a low profile. "Party weekend," I say, nodding, trying out my "enthusiastic look."

"Don't I know it!" Either the look's pure gold or Chris/Jose is pure clueless. "Paper or plastic?"

LATER TUESDAY AFTERNOON: DETAIL #3

"I got your note," says Noah. "Way to be old school, having Mattia deliver it during calculus."

I stop packing the groceries in my pink gym duffel and readjust my phone, which is slipping off my shoulder. "And?"

"Kudos on not leaving your phone number, by the way," he goes on, like I didn't say anything. "Very PI, very hard to trace, et cetera. You're lucky I even bothered tracking it down. Oh, and expect a call from Mattia."

"So are we on?" I ask, shoving some packages of fruit snacks to fill the extra space between my clothes. "I'm very busy here, you know."

"I'm sure you are," Noah says. Sometimes I'm thankful for the phone world, where I don't have to see everybody's body language when they talk. I can imagine Noah rolling his eyes, scoffing. But thanks to my being nowhere near him, I can just as easily imagine him looking all excited and on board.

"I'm taking that as a yes," I say. "So Thursday morning, pick me up at seven o' clock." It pains me to say it, but I have to be practical. "We have a solid ten-hour drive and we want to get there before it's too dark. I'll be waiting for you on my front porch."

"Yes, ma'am," he says, and because I can imagine him any way I want to, I picture him saluting.

LATEST TUESDAY AFTERNOON: DETAIL #3, REVISITED

"What phone plan on this good green earth doesn't have call waiting?" Mattia calls exactly two-point-one seconds after I hang up with Noah. "That was him, right? What did he want?"

"Hi, Mattia. I'm fine, thanks, how are you?"

"Seriously, Joy. I gave Noah that note this morning. Did I open it first? *No.* Did I ask questions? *No.* I was but your humble messenger."

I groan and fall onto my bed. "And I thanked you."

"Then," she continues, "after class, Noah asked me for your number. Did I ask why he wanted it? *No.* Did I mock him about being into you? *No.* Again, I simply delivered the requested information."

"And I bet *he* thanked you, too."

"I don't want thanks, I want answers. And I want them now."

I sigh, slowly sitting up. "It's not a phone kind of conversation."

"Fine. Tomorrow on the way to school."

"It's not a way-to-school conversation, either."

"What kind of conversation is it?"

It's a let's-not-have-it-at-all kind of conversation, and I'm trying to put that tactfully when Mattia says: "Okay, I've got it. Sleepover tomorrow. Just you and me, to kick off the superlong weekend. And you can let me in on all your juicy but conflicted feelings toward Noah."

How sad is it that Mattia uses the term "conflicted feelings" in about half of her conversations? "Sorry, I can't," I say.

"Why not?"

"Plans."

"Can you be a little more vague?"

"Plans to go to Claremont. I'm making a campus visit."

"Without me?"

"You said you didn't want to go!" I *so* don't want to get into this. Mentally, I recalculate. "Fine, we'll have a sleepover."

"Okay, okay, don't sound so excited." Mattia is thoroughly confused, like *I'm* the one being all codependent. "See you tomorrow morning, right? Minus the attitude."

"Okay," I say, shaking my head.

I need a vacation.

THIS I BELIEVE

In English sophomore year I had to write an essay called "This I Believe."

It was based on some idea from National Public Radio, where people wrote in about their beliefs. The essays weren't necessarily supposed to be about your religious beliefs, but mine was.

Because the thing is I do believe. I believe in God, and I believe in Jesus Christ, and I believe in my religion. I go to church every week, pray every day, read the Book of Mormon and the Bible. I don't drink alcohol, tea, coffee—even caffeinated soda.

I believe in waiting, so I'm okay with the rules— nothing even *resembling* sex until I'm married. No dating before the age of sixteen, no wearing clothes that might give guys the wrong idea, being very careful with kisses—I believe all of that. I believe in repentance, forgiveness, integrity.

Even now that I live in a town where it's hard to tell where belief ends and culture begins—I don't like the culture, but I do like the belief. That was never an issue with me. It was too late before I realized it was an issue with Zan.

ONE LAST THING

It's never just one thing. If it were, U.S. history would be a two-week course, not something you study your whole life. The Civil War wasn't just about slavery, and the Revolutionary War wasn't just about freedom. World War I wasn't just because some guy got assassinated, and World War II wasn't just because of Nazis, and the Beatles didn't break up just because of Yoko Ono. It's never just one thing.

That's how it was with Zan leaving. Zan leaving high school, Zan leaving Haven, Zan leaving me. It wasn't just one big, concrete thing. He didn't stop loving me. He didn't stop believing in the church. That's too easy, and too easy isn't Zan. Zan's never simple.

Instead, it's just bits and pieces that I try to put together into a story that makes sense.

I remember that Sunday last summer. Zan and I usually didn't go to church together since we lived in different wards, but that day was different because Greg Weyland, a guy in my ward who'd just graduated, was leaving on a mission to Brazil. Greg would be delivering his farewell address in church, and I persuaded Zan to come with me, even though he didn't even know Greg that well.

I remember sharing a church pew with Zan, his white shirt wrinkle-free and spotless, his navy tie crisp against it. I remember the sacrament tray moving from hand to hand down the bench, everyone taking a cube of bread before passing it along. We swallowed it in quiet reflection, or at least in an attempt at quiet reflection since between the occasional baby's scream and toddler's tantrum there were a lot of interruptions.

And Zan handed me the tray without letting it linger over his lap. Not that I was supposed to notice. Taking the sacrament was personal, not something anyone should look at or judge. But I'd noticed, and he hadn't taken it, and why? The only reason you don't take the sacrament is if you're unworthy.

My heart started pumping ice-blood, the way it did whenever I was terrified, or just really cold. Zan said it was physically impossible for a mammal to produce ice-blood, but I told him science was always wrong, anyway, so why wouldn't it be wrong about ice-blood?

I looked at him but kept my head bowed so he wouldn't notice. Nothing in his face told his secret. Sure, he wasn't freshly shaven—the scruff around his chin had grown past the pokey stage, into the long, soft stage my legs sometimes got to when I hadn't shaved all winter. It was customary for men to shave before church (most men in Haven didn't even have beards or mustaches) but it was just cultural. It didn't have anything to do with our religion, not really.

I thought about our trips to the Sev, just off the freeway outside of Haven. It was a trucker exit, mainly; nothing was out there but oil refineries and the lone 7-Eleven. Everybody else hung out at DQ, which was why we didn't.

I'd get a piña colada Slurpee, or maybe a cherry/orange hybrid. He'd started ordering Mocha Java, a definite Mormon no-no no matter where you lived, but I didn't mind. I figured the coffee had less to do with a crisis of faith and more to do with Zan flipping off Haven culture in his usual over-the-top style.

But what if it went deeper than that? And if it did, why hadn't he told me? He told me everything. Didn't he?

And I remember that night, after church, when he invited me to the Sev one last time. And it was so late and too dark, and there were mosquitoes out, lots of them, because it was late, but not cold, and dark, but not still. I remember that night in flashes, like a dream you remember some of, but not all, so you're not sure whether it's a dream or if it actually happened and just *felt* like a dream.

It was real, though. Every day I live with how real it was.

All I remember is the one line he kept saying: "I have to get away from this. All of this." And my mind must know he said other things. My mind must hold them tight in its deepest creases. Because all my ears know, all my eyes know, all my heart knows is that he had to get away from this. All of this.

It's never just one thing. It's a combination of things so small that if they weren't all stacked together nothing would change at all. Small things stacked on top of each other made him leave, but I wasn't one of them, was I?

Was I?

WEDNESDAY NIGHT

I come to Mattia's house with a sleeping bag, a weekend's worth of clothes, and a convenience-store-in-a-duffel.

As I expect, she doesn't notice. Instead she says, "I was wondering when you'd get here!" as we head downstairs to her bedroom.

I'm late because I had to call Noah with the new plan. I don't tell Mattia this.

Mattia has a huge bedroom, the "second master" with its own bathroom, a walk-in closet, and a window seat wide enough—and just barely long enough—for me to sleep on. I love the window seat, plus it has the added benefit of being on the ground level. I've told Noah to knock on the window tomorrow morning instead of honking or ringing the doorbell, so as not to arouse suspicion.

"Okay," she says. "Now that we're here alone, in person, without any interruptions, will you finally tell me about what's up with you and Noah?"

I start unrolling my sleeping bag. "There's nothing to tell about me and Noah. He's just like . . ." What is he just like? He's not just like anything, or anyone. "I still don't like him," I finally say, which is, for the most part, true.

"Riiight," she says, glancing over at my makeshift bed. "Come on. We're going on a walk." Only now do I notice her hair's braided and she's wearing a pair of trendy-but-not-too-trendy athletic pants.

"Now?" I say, yawning.

Mattia raises an eyebrow. "It's eight thirty." She lifts up a corner of her bed skirt to reveal a pair of Nikes. "Noah lives a few streets over. I figured we could casually walk by his house while you fill me in on things. Like when we do drive-bys, except on foot."

Drive-bys. We do them for the guys anyone in our group likes. Or the guys Mattia thinks we should like. We've driven past the houses of about a dozen guys she's seen as potential prospects for one of us.

We drove past Zan's. We were crammed into the Rabbit and we laughed, and we kept the windows down and the radio up. I saw a lit window and wondered if it was his; wondered if he was thinking of me.

"We're not doing some drive-by/walk-by for Noah. Drive-bys are reserved for guys who hold romantic promise."

"Um, yeah. Like Noah."

"No."

"Then why did he call you yesterday? Don't try to lie. I already know it was about something important, or you would have told me about it long ago." She stops tying her shoe and stares at me. This is the most attention I've had from her, like, ever.

"Okay, fine. Here it is: tomorrow morning I'm going to Claremont. With Noah. He needed my number so we could discuss the details." I'm expecting an explosion and Mattia does not disappoint.

"You're going to Claremont with Noah and not me?" she shrieks. Then her face drains of color and she repeats it, slower and softer. "You're going to Claremont with Noah and not me. Because you want to see Zan. This isn't a college visit at all, is it? You're not going to Claremont— you're going to see Zan."

She makes it sound like I've been lying to her. "No, I *am* going to Claremont. And we are going on a college visit. And we're going to find Zan there."

"*Find* Zan? Why? Zan doesn't need to be found. You already know where he is. You're going there to stalk him!"

"I'm going there to help him!" He needs to remember what he left behind when he took off. He needs to remember *me.*

"He doesn't want your help! Face it, Joy. Zan doesn't love you. He probably never did. You couldn't convince him to stay. You couldn't convince him to take you with him. He wanted a clean break." It's obvious she thinks I'm part of what he was breaking away from. "I'm sorry to have to be the one to tell you this, but Zan is gone."

"Zan is not gone and you are not sorry," I say, picking up my sleeping bag. "Zan is in California, living out his dreams, and I intend to remind him that I'm a part of them. Starting tomorrow."

She closes her eyes, and then opens them. "You don't understand what a huge mistake this is."

"You don't understand why I have to do it whether it's a mistake or not! I have to get out of here. I have to find Zan. If I don't try to get him back, I'll spend my whole life drowning in regret."

"Regret, huh? Let me tell you something about regret. Regret is spending your senior year pining after some geek who would rather make up a crazy language and ride a bicycle than be with you!" Mattia stands and turns away from me, walking straight into the depths of her closet.

"Listen to what I'm telling you." I say each word slowly. "I. Need. Closure."

Mattia emerges from her closet, pulling an Old Navy hoodie over her head, and storms out of the room. "You want closure?" she asks me, eyes narrowed. "*This* is closure." The door slams behind her.

"That's classic passive-aggressive behavior!" I yell through the door. They're words she's used to describe the actions of guys, celebrities, the assistant principal. They're her own words, parroted back to her.

And still she isn't hearing me.

READY TO DO THIS THING

It's still dark outside when Noah taps on the window, so I can't see him. I only know it's him because he taps the same way he knocks: three short, three long, then three more short.

I've got only the dim light from Mattia's desk lamp to work with, so I hope Noah sees me signal to him that I'll be out in a minute. His face looks almost sinister against the sky's shadows. It's just Noah. But my ice-blood still won't slow down.

Mattia can, and does, sleep through anything. She's snoring, oblivious to the fact that I'm leaving, oblivious that this trip will change both our lives forever. She's content to stay here. I have to go after what's important to me. Thoughts of leaving her a note vanish. What would a note solve?

I slip out the sliding glass door into the cold morning. The SAAB's already running, keeping warm. The hatchback's wide open. "Hey." I'm surprised it's cold enough that I can see my breath, and his.

"Good morning." He starts packing in my bags without me asking. "Ready to do this thing?"

"Ready as I'll ever be." For the briefest of seconds, it hits me that we're really leaving. For the briefest of seconds, my stomach shrieks out, "Wait!"

I bite the inside of my lower lip. "This is the right thing to do, right Noah?"

He opens the car door for me. "This is the thing we're doing, whether it's right or not." He smiles. "Buckle up."

HOUR ONE

The problem with long car trips is that they give you lots of time to think. I'd prefer not to have all this time to think right now.

For one thing, my brain can't function right before eight o'clock in the morning. It's just the way I'm wired. I change my schedule every year so that I have keyboarding or financial literacy or some other no-sequential-thinking-required class first thing in the morning.

Then there's the reality that thoughts of Zan never leave my mind even on days when I have no shortage of annoying tidbits to monopolize my mind. An empty, blank morning like this one is just asking for trouble.

Asking for trouble. Maybe that's why I feel like I'm in a getaway car, doing something illegal. But we won't get pulled over. We aren't doing anything wrong.

Noah looks like he wants to say something, but he's quiet.

I wonder if he's mad. Or sad. Or thinking I'm stupid.

I wish I knew what he was thinking. I hate that I wish I knew what he was thinking.

"So." Noah fiddles with the radio, which is placed abnormally high on the dashboard. "You nervous?"

"Aren't you?" The only things Noah's finding us are early-morning news reports and ads for home refinancing. "Here, I'll do that." I motion to the radio.

"I guess I'm a little bit . . . apprehensive," he says, his full attention now on the road. "Apprehensive, but not nervous."

"What's the difference?" I arbitrarily flip through a country song.

"Hey, leave it there," says Noah. "I like that song."

"You're a country fan?"

"Apprehension is excitement and wariness combined."

"Wariness?" Something about the word doesn't sound right. Maybe it's just because of my fuzzy head.

"Yes, I'm a country fan!" He explodes, pounding one fist on the wheel. "So sue me, okay?"

Wow. Is that my imagination or is Noah Talbot, King of Calm 'n' Cool, totally losing it? Maybe I'm making things up. I am pretty tired. Now that all the preparing-for-the-great-getaway action is over, I have a chance to remember how little sleep I've gotten in the past week.

"Listen, there's no shame in listening to country music. If you have no pride, at least." I yawn. "Sorry. It just slipped out. Forgive me." Need sleep.

"I'm sorry, too." Unlike me, Noah looks genuinely sorry. "Rush hour traffic stresses me out."

Finally, common ground. "Me too," I say. "Me too."

PEOPLE ASK ME WHAT
I MISS MOST

People ask me what I miss most about California, and what I miss most is what I never had. In California, I never had a Spanish-style ranch house, with smooth, clean stucco walls and copper-colored tile on the roof, orange trees shading the front yard.

I never had this. I miss it anyway.

HOUR THREE

There is whistling. I can't make out the tune, but there is whistling, and it is getting louder.

I can feel the daylight penetrate my lids before I open my eyes. "How long was I asleep?" I ask, rubbing my eyes.

The whistling stops. "Maybe an hour or so." Like Zan, Noah stares straight ahead while he drives.

I rub my eyes again and blink a few times to get a clear view out the window. The landscape just looks dirty, with some sagebrush rolling around. Not exactly postcard-perfect. "When do we get to the scenery?"

"You're looking at it," says Noah.

That's when I notice it. "What are you wearing?"

Noah's eyebrows knot. "Uh, clothes?"

"On your head, idiot."

A smile takes over his face, and he touches his head. "Oh, you mean this." He lifts his hat and gives it to me.

It's one of those tacky, trucker-style baseball caps with an adjustable plastic band and a wide brim. "Ick, what is this?"

"Just read the front." Noah grins wider.

There, embroidered in red thread: DON'T FORGET MY SENIOR DISCOUNT!

"Sweet, eh? I found out about it when I was recycling newspapers. You know, mixed in with the Sunday morning ads? I got one for my whole crew. We wear 'em with pride, just like the ad said to."

And I believe this. Without question.

"Yeah, but the ad is for *senior citizens*. It's just wrong wearing a hat designed for the elderly." I stick it back on his head, smooshing his hair. A few strands escape, and they're soft under my skin.

Noah's hair feels just like hair that gorgeous should feel. He's not like one of those guys who look good from a distance, but when you get up close you notice his hair is all crunchy with product or he has teeny-tiny zits at the top of his forehead. "A country fan wearing an old-man hat. Pathetic."

But I'm thinking of Zan, how he wore his grandpa's loafers. How I go for the guys who go old-school. Not that I'm going for Noah. So he's hot. So? I've always known he was hot. It doesn't mean anything that I'm noticing again now. We're sitting right next to each other, after all. Proximity.

I rummage through my backpack. I don't know what

I'm looking for, but I have to turn my attention away from Noah, from his soft hair and old-man hat.

"You're just jealous," Noah says. "You wish you were in my crew so you could wear one, too."

"Have I not made it abundantly clear how little I want to be in your crew?"

"Yeah, but I know you're lying."

I groan. "Because everybody wants to be in your crew, right?"

"Everybody with good taste." Noah grins.

"Good taste? You guys wear Senior Discount hats and dance around the school like you're in some Disney Channel movie."

Noah starts shaking his head before I even finish talking. "We don't dance. I don't like dancing."

I hope he can see me roll my eyes. "Yeah, and nobody would *dare* do something you don't like."

"My friends wouldn't." He pauses. "Or at least most of them."

And Noah and I, we stop talking. We are thinking of Zan. We are haunted by Zan.

PEOPLE ASK ME WHAT
I MISS MOST

People ask me what I miss most about California, and what I miss most is what I never had. In California, I never had a boyfriend at one of the colleges, one who took Modern Chinese Literature and Political Psychology, and didn't care that I took French II and eleventh-grade English. I miss hanging out with him in the village, eating chocolate-dipped s'mores and browsing used books. I miss him holding out a daylily, yellow bleeding into orange like a perfectly ripe nectarine, saying it's almost as beautiful as I am.

I never had this. I miss it anyway.

TOWNS WE PASS

Beaver

Sulphurdale

Browse

Paragonah

Toquerville

HOUR FOUR

It's not really lunchtime yet, but since it wasn't really breakfast yet when we left, I figure it's time to break out the snacks. I open the Chips Ahoy!, a bag of Doritos, and two bottles of Sprite. Noah drives, occasionally using shorthand like, "Chips, please," or "Drink."

I wish he wasn't so hell-bent on getting good gas mileage. According to him, driving behind a semi makes for good fuel economy, and we've been crawling along at sixty miles an hour. *You're driving a turbo,* I want to say. I'm still not positive what that means, but I'm pretty sure his mileage is already shot. *Live it up, man. Go seventy-five.* Instead I say: "This classic has no tunes."

Noah sighs, exasperated. "That isn't the car's fault. We're driving through the middle of nowhere, so we don't have any radio."

"A car from the current century would pick up at least one or two stations."

A slow smile spreads across his face. "Yeah, but

would a car from the current century have *this*?" He smiles wider now, and taps just below the clock. A cassette tape deck.

"Nice." I give him a thumbs-up. "I haven't seen one of those since I used to ride around with my grandma." Back when she still drove, Grandma had a huge white car that spoke to her. A little mechanical voice would tell her things: *Please fasten your seat belt. Your windshield wiper fluid is low. A door is ajar.* Grandma would listen to books on tape. If Noah has books on tape I hope they aren't lame mysteries that you figure out thirty minutes into it. Those ruin the whole drive. "So do you have any tapes?"

"Feast your eyes on this." He takes one hand off the wheel and takes a zippered case from the console. "Sweet, eh?"

I unzip, and all the tapes are in a row, plastic cases spine-up. "Kris Kross, Tiffany, Wilson Phillips? Who are these people?"

"Keep going." Noah's excited, like a little kid showing off a baseball-card collection. "There's a New Kids on the Block album from when they were popular the first time."

"Um, New Kids on the Block has never been popular a second time."

"Oh, they will be. Just you wait."

"Yeah, I'll be holding my breath." I keep flipping through titles. "Man, your musical taste is appalling. Country, forgettable eighties pop . . . Barry Manilow? No way!"

"That one's my mom's. She doesn't have a tape player and she—"

This is awesome. "I love Barry Manilow!"

Noah winces. "Don't admit that in public. Or if you do, sound at least a little bit ashamed."

"But I'm not at least a little bit ashamed. Barry rocks!" I pull open the case and try to slip the tape into his right hand, but it's a no-go.

"You want to listen to it, you put it in." He keeps both hands on the wheel, both eyes on the road.

"I don't know how. I've never used one of these." I don't mention that even Grandma's tape deck was newer than this one. No need to be catty.

"You just slide it in. It's not hard." He pumps his fist in a little cheer. "You can do it!"

Zan wouldn't make me do it. Zan would just do it for me. That's the kind of boyfriend he is. Was. Will be. Whatever.

But Zan's not here, Noah is. So I accidentally force the tape in backward once, realize it's not happening, and flip the tape over so it feeds smoothly into the deck. On the tape Barry is midway through "Copacabana," and I sing along. In my imagination, it's Zan sitting next to me, not Noah. In my imagination, Zan is joining in with me on the chorus.

BARRY SONGS THAT REMIND ME OF ZAN

Can't Smile Without You

The Old Songs

Looks Like We Made It

HOUR FIVE

"Don't you think Zan looks like Barry Manilow?"

"No."

"Not the current Barry Manilow. The Barry Manilow of the seventies. He and Zan had the same shaggy, feathery hair."

"Didn't the Barry Manilow of the seventies also have a gigantic nose?" says Noah.

I just pretend like he agrees with me. "Those thick, soulful eyebrows, too. They're just like Zan's."

"Zan doesn't look like Barry Manilow, past, present, or future. Will you please just quit talking about Barry Manilow? And will you please, please, *please* quit talking about Zan?"

Noah sounds annoyed, which makes me annoyed. I'm cool with ticking him off, but not if it's at Zan's expense. Or Barry's. I eject the tape from the deck. "Look, in just a couple of hours we're going to be in the same city as Zan. Now's the time to start remembering things about him."

Noah just drives for a long time. But I still don't care

if he's mad. Even if his silence does make me uncomfortable without Barry's soothing tones to fill in the gaps. Finally he says, "I remember stuff about him. I just don't feel like sharing everything I remember with you."

"Well, share away! I'm all about sharing the Zanories. That's my newly created word for Zan memories, by the way."

"Yeah, I caught that." Noah pushes harder on the gas pedal. "The first time I met you was because of Zan. Your birthday party last year." We're definitely going faster now, and I watch his hands flex on the steering wheel. "Remember?"

"Of course I remember. You brought me my present from Zan." I pretend like I don't notice our rapid increase in speed. Maybe this is what the pizza guy meant by "turbo." Why Noah's using this SAAB superpower now, when the trip's practically over, is one of his many not-that-interesting mysteries.

"You know what Zan gave me?" I ask, because it occurs to me that he might not. "A blank book for writing poetry. It was spiral-bound and covered in purple velvet." I know they're unnecessary details, but I like the way it shows he has no taste, but that he knows me. Knew me.

"His mother bought it," says Noah wryly. "Wrote the card, too."

PEOPLE ASK ME WHAT
I MISS MOST

People ask me what I miss most about California, and what I miss most is what I never had. In California, I never had an entire summer at Huntington Beach, every single shade of sand slipping through my fingers, between my toes, in my hair. I miss my feet making prints in the cakey, just-moistened sand, or gliding over it, solid and compact, at the ocean's edge. I never had a little brother, skin the color of a nude nylon, eyes the color of Zan's, tottering along the beach with a plastic pail collecting seashells.

I never had any of them. I miss them anyway.

HOUR NINE

"So I've been wondering something."

"Something I know the answer to?" Noah takes his eyes off the road for a full nanosecond to look at me. Probably because we've been silent so long. I've forgotten how much time has passed since anybody spoke.

"Something you, and only you, know the answer to," I say. "Which is this: Why are you antilove?"

Noah's eyebrows scrunch up. "What makes you think I'm antilove? What does that even mean?"

"You tell me. You're the one who doesn't believe in having a girlfriend in high school."

He finishes making a gradual turn and then we're staring straight into the sun. I flip down the visor in front of my seat. The brightness is unexpected. Still, it feels like he's cheating when he puts his sunglasses on. I want to know what he's thinking, and I need all the clues I can get.

"Deciding not to have a girlfriend isn't the same as being antilove," he says, like it's obvious. "Just because two people are a couple doesn't mean they're in love. In fact, most of the time they aren't. Especially in high school."

"Sometimes they are, though. Sometimes two people are drawn to each other by a force greater than themselves. And sometimes that happens in high school."

"Like with you and Zan?" I'm beginning to notice a pattern in how Noah speaks. He says everything in basically the same tone: a calm, noncommittal tone that doesn't portray any emotion. So he might be sarcastic when he says it or he might be totally sincere. I don't know, so I can't get mad at him.

"We're not talking about me and Zan. We're talking about you being antilove."

"I'm not antilove! I just think high school relationships are dumb."

"Because you don't want to get too attached before your mission. Because you don't want to risk actually caring about a girl." I don't know why I'm getting irritated, but I am. "You don't want her to get all needy and send you letters and care packages every day when you're gone."

"I wouldn't mind the care packages," he says all jokey, smiling.

It only makes me madder. I want to know the truth about this. I don't know why I'm taking it so seriously, but I want him to, too. "When you fall in love, you can't help it. It's not something you can put off, just because you've decided you should."

Noah shrugs. "Maybe you're right. But that's never happened to me. So I don't worry that it will."

"But what if it *does*?" I prod. And again, I don't know why.

And again, he makes a joke. "Are you falling in love with me, Joy Afterclein?"

"It's the Senior Discount hat that did it," I deadpan. "Irresistible."

In the distance, clouds are stretched so low in the sky they reach right to the mountains. Somewhere, it is raining. The strange sun makes me feel like an actor in a movie, caught between light and dark. I wish the Barry tape was still providing background music.

"I believe in love," Noah says finally. "I just haven't figured it out yet."

Why is hearing him say it a relief? It is, though. I feel some part of me, somewhere, unclench. "I've got it even less figured out than you, probably. I'm learning the hard way."

"And I'm here learning the hard way with you."

Maybe he wants it to sound reassuring, but it just sounds stupid. "Yeah, you are. Idiot."

CITIES WE PASS

Corona

Norco

Mira Loma

Rancho Cucamonga

Upland

GRETEL'S HOUSE

You know how people say pets resemble their owner? To me, Gretel has always resembled her house. I mean, not on the surface: she's a willowy seventeen-year-old with light brown hair, light brown skin, and amber-colored eyes. Her house is a ninety-four-year-old Craftsman with extra-wide front doors, cool old light fixtures, and stained glass.

But the house looks like the kind of fairy-tale cottage a girl named Gretel would live in. Like Gretel, it's full of built-in hidden treasures—the tiny bench between the staircase and the living-room wall, the bookshelves popping out from unexpected places, the ceiling beams slanting at unusual angles. Her house smells of jasmine.

I open the car door. Even though it's evening, the air is soft, like velvet. It's nothing like the hard Haven air, always stinging you with icy cold or blistering heat. Noah feels it, too, because he breathes in long and deep while he stretches his legs.

"Joy!" Gretel runs up to me, and her hair is much,

much longer than it used to be and she hugs me hard and says, "It's so good to see you!" She breaks away from me and extends her hand, all grace and poise. Everything I'm not. Everything I've missed. "You must be Noah. Pleased to meet you."

"Yeah, hey," Noah mumbles back, his hair flopping in his face just enough that I know he's ducked his head. Noah? Shy? Maybe it's Gretel. Maybe her charm and beauty affect even Soccer Lovin' Kids.

"So, let's get your stuff so we can eat!" says Gretel. "You guys must be *starving*." She opens the back door and takes out our snack bag, eyeing the soda and cookies carefully but without showing any judgment. "We're having mac and cheese made with whole grain pasta," she says, looking at Noah. "I hope you're okay with that. We're vegetarian."

Noah lifts his head. "That's cool," he says, and smiles.

THE CONVERSATION
GRETEL AND I HAVE
INSTEAD OF PLAYING UNO

Noah gets the guest room, and I'm bunking with Gretel, just like back in the good old days. I love Gretel's room, with its hardwood floors and funky patchwork quilt and handwoven area rug. I've never found a bedroom remotely like hers in Haven. I breathe in the same way Noah did when we first got here: long, hard, and audible.

"You happy to see me or something?" Gretel unrolls my sleeping bag and I am reminded of unrolling my sleeping bag last night. I'd known that girl for a few months.

I've known this girl for as long as I can remember. We were from the handful of Mormon families in town, and we went to the church nursery together as toddlers, the church Primary together as children, and the church Young Women together up until last year.

"I'm thrilled to see you or something," I say, examining my reflection in the mirror she framed herself, out of triangular pieces of glass in all different colors. Gretel goes to fine arts camp every year, and she made the mirror the last summer before she became a counselor.

When I look at myself, I'm expecting red-rimmed eyes and pasty skin after a day of driving and a dinner with the Addison family. But instead I see something in my eyes I haven't seen in a long time. Something that makes them brighter—brighter and softer both.

Gretel finishes straightening the sleeping bag, tosses one of her pillows on it with a flourish, and sits, cross-legged, on the bed. "You promised to give me all the details when you got here," she says. "So spill."

"Not now. I don't want to leave Noah alone in a strange house. Let's go play Uno or something." Uno is, of course, the lamest game known to man. Must be why it feels like exactly the right game to play with Noah.

Gretel rolls her eyes. "First off, Uno? Um, no. Second, Noah wanted some 'chill time,' as he put it. The drive exhausted him."

It sounds like a made-up story to convince me to gossip with her. "And when exactly did he tell you all this?"

"After dinner, while you were chatting it up with my parents. He and I were doing the dishes. He's a much better houseguest than you are, by the way."

I'm less than thrilled by this information. "Terrif. So what'd you guys discuss?"

"Very little, actually. That guy's loyal to you to a fault."

I sigh. "It's not just me. Noah's loyal to everybody. It's his thing. His all-around-great-guy self."

"Well, it's boring. Whenever I asked him about the trip, about you, about the two of you, he was totally vague." She brushes a strand of hair out of her face.

"You asked him about *the two of us*? No wonder he was vague—he's probably totally freaked out because he thinks I told you there was a two of us and now he has to tactfully tell me how wrong I am so he can remain his all-around-great-guy self." This is so not good. "Why would you say that? You *know* there's not a two of us."

"Just how would I know that?" Gretel asks, pounding her fists on the mattress like she's done a hundred times before. That's just counting when she's mad at *me*. "You haven't told me anything about why you're here except that you need closure. Noah, however, seems like a normal guy who does not need closure. So the question is, why did he just drive all day and agree to stay with some family he's never met before?"

I think about how to answer this while taking my prized Barry Manilow concert tee out of my bag. I've never seen Barry live—the shirt is an older-than-I-am relic from my mom's college days. It's paper-thin and ragged at the collar, but I sleep in it almost every night. Pulling it over my head, I say: "Driving all day wasn't a big deal to him. He's a car person. That's his car out there. A SAAB nine hundred. A classic."

"Just because he has a classic car and likes to drive it doesn't mean he wants to drive it to *Claremont*, of all places. Jeez, Joy, you're really not a car person, are you?" It's obviously a rhetorical question. "This whole thing is really strange."

"Yeah, but my whole life is really strange, so I'm okay with it." While Gretel changes for the night, I turn my head and stare into the mirror again. I like the way I look. I look like who I used to be. "This whole thing is just one more part of my Haven world that defies all natural laws. But I'm here now. So can we just leave that world behind?"

All Gretel's wearing are snowflake-patterned pajama pants and a party-pink bra from Victoria's Secret, her one corporate sellout. "Yeah," she says finally, nodding. "Yeah, we can."

I didn't realize it until now, but I'm exhausted, so I slide into my sleeping bag while Gretel pulls on a graphic tee for some indie band, probably a local one. It's too bad I hate camping, I think, feeling the fake-silkiness beneath me. When I'm indoors, I love my sleeping bag.

All is right in this world. I'm in my cozy sleeping bag, with my best friend who supports the arts and indie rock, and I'm going to find my boyfriend and get the answers I deserve. The answers are going to fit together, make sense. How can they not? Everything makes sense here, tonight.

Except Noah. He's the only thing that doesn't fit together, make sense. Gretel's right: this, all of this, is really strange. And I was telling the truth when I told her I was okay with it, because there's no denying that my whole life is strange.

But Noah's isn't. Noah's UEA break is supposed to consist of fun, wholesome recreation, like visiting the pumpkin patch with the other Soccer Lovin' Kids, going on hayrides and flirting with girls by throwing straw in their hair. It's almost scary how clearly I can see Noah's alterna-UEA break play out in my mind, like a video that was shot but never uploaded.

So far his real UEA break's been so dull it couldn't even be a documentary: driving all day with some random girl he feels sorry for, staying with strangers because he feels obligated. I think back to today, the good parts, and how they were probably only good for him because they meant he succeeded.

Hurt—a heavy, dull hurt—sinks in piece-by-piece, and the fake-silkiness turns cold beneath my legs, and all is not right with the world. The realization is like a double punch to the gut, taking away the happiness I feel now *and* the happiness I felt today. I am his service project. I am nothing more.

I knew that. I knew that all along, really. So why am I letting it bother me now? Noah doesn't want to be here, but who cares? He doesn't make sense here anyway, and everything else does. The way I do. The way I do with my boyfriend.

My boyfriend. Who is not Noah. Zan. Zan's the one who matters. I want that thought, right there, to counteract every hurt I'm feeling. It doesn't, though. But it does start to fade.

"Wait," Gretel says. "You're not seriously getting into bed right now, are you?"

"Uh, no?"

"I invited Tess and Jen over. Just to kick back, nothing fancy or anything. Is that okay?"

"You invited Tess and Jen over? Now?"

Gretel gives me a weird look. "It's eight thirty."

Whoa. Flashback.

It's not that I don't want to see Tess and Jen. After all, they're my peeps, my posse, my friends-till-the-end. I guess I just didn't plan on seeing them until later. Later, when I had Zan back. Later, when things were right again and I wouldn't look like such a loser.

But friends are supposed to see you at your most pathetic. Friends are supposed to see you at your bottom-of-the-barrel worst and love you anyway. And you're supposed to let them.

"Okay," I say, sliding out of my sleeping bag and feeling warmer immediately. "When are they getting here?"

FEMALE BONDING

It's crazy how some people you can see every day and you still aren't comfortable talking to them, but others you go without talking to for months and in nine seconds it's like no time has passed.

Tess's got her MacBook flipped open and is sprawled perpendicular to me on the floor. It looks the same as the one she had when I left—white and skinny—but knowing Tess, it's a safe bet that this is a newer, faster, superior version. I say, "Nice computer," and she rattles off stuff about giggers and hard drives that she must know I don't understand a word of. I love how familiar she sounds, how familiar she looks with her black-brown hair lanky around her chunky, college-girl glasses. Not that she's actually in college, but in spirit Tess has been in college her whole life. It's just who she is.

Jen's curled up in a corner of Gretel's four-poster bed, knitting. Her hands move so fast they almost look like they're shaking, and there's an ever-shrinking ball of teal-colored yarn at her feet. "So, should I be offended you didn't tell me you were coming?" she asks, half smiling, half curious.

"Yeah," says Tess. "You didn't tell me, either. Should I feel left out?"

"The trip was totally last minute."

"She barely even told me she was coming," Gretel adds.

"Again, *last minute.*"

"Okay, so what exactly sparked this impromptu visit?" Jen looks right at me, her gray eyes skeptical and catlike. Her needles don't slow even for a second.

Jen's been knitting ever since I met her. I mean, she's stopped to sleep and go to school and stuff, but if she can be doing two things at once, she is, and one of them is usually knitting. Apparently she went to this überprogressive elementary school, where this was actually part of the curriculum. Maybe they're onto something—Jen can focus on two things at once better than I can focus on one thing at once.

"You know," I tell her, "the girls in Haven are way into crafts, too. You'd fit in really well there."

"Dude, do *not* say that." Jen shakes her head. "I want no connection to that town or any of its . . ." She struggles for the words. "Its . . . things." She looks disgusted, and I can't tell whether it's because of Haven or because she couldn't come up with a better word than "things."

"You're changing the subject, Joy," says Tess.

"Yeah, answer my question!" Jen says. "Why was it so important to get here pronto that you couldn't even give your friends a heads-up first?"

"Zan." This time when I yawn I don't bother hiding it. "Zan can't wait."

Tess and Jen both nod, and I'm relieved for my real friends, the ones who know me, the ones who know that's all there is to it. Until Gretel says, "Oh, and she brought one of her Haven things with her."

HAVEN THING

"*If we must* do this," I say, rummaging through my backpack, "then at least let me change out of my Barry shirt first." The striped Henley I was wearing all day doesn't really go with my pajama pants, but I don't want to change clothes entirely and have my friends think that I think this late-night visit to his room is a big deal. But I don't want to wear my Barry shirt, either, and make myself look like an even bigger service project than Noah already thinks I am—a lunatic Barry Manilow fan who drags some guy who couldn't care less to her old hometown and makes him meet her friends.

"If we *must*? Of course we must! I can't believe you thought you could sneak a hot guy on this trip without even telling us." Jen pulls a Dr Pepper Lip Smacker out of her pocket.

"How do you know he's hot?"

"He sounds hot," says Tess.

"How can he sound hot? You haven't heard his voice.

You haven't heard a physical description of him. You haven't heard anything about him at all."

"Methinks the lady doth protest too much," Gretel says, "and you really do want to go in and wish him good night." The guest room, where Noah's staying, is next to the kitchen, so Gretel's come up with the plan to go downstairs for a snack and casually "say hi."

"I do not. I just want to go to sleep. It's after midnight."

"Dude," says Jen, rolling her eyes again, "it's nine thirty."

"Ten thirty my time!"

Tess closes her computer. "Okay, even I think that's lame. Let's go."

I try to make sure the stairs don't creak on my way down, but I'm the only one who does. "Guys, can you be a little quieter?" I whisper.

"Why are you whispering?" Jen exaggerates tiptoeing in her hand-knit red slipper socks. "Nobody's asleep yet."

Gretel flips on a light over the kitchen sink. "There's soda in the fridge."

I can't help a smile sneaking into my eyes. "Do you have any Sprite?"

"We have an all-natural lemon-lime alternative to Sprite." She lifts a bag of organic cookies off a shelf in the pantry. "Does that count?"

"You're a Sprite drinker now?" asks Tess, getting herself a can of something that looks berry flavor.

"Nope, but Noah is."

"You know his beverage preferences?" Jen raises an eyebrow. "This is getting serious."

"It is not! Get me a can of whatever you're having," I tell Tess.

"Let me ask you this, then," Gretel says, turning out the light. "Do you even know *Zan's* favorite drink?"

It's dark now, dark enough that I know she can't see my face as it crumples, thinking of Mocha Java. "Yes. Yes I do."

"Room service!" Gretel says, tapping on Noah's door.

As he opens it, the dim hallway is slowly bathed in apple juice–colored light.

Besides the bedside lamp being on, Noah's room looks uninhabited—the bed is unmussed and his stuff must be hidden in his closet. His iPod is clipped to his track pants, but he probably wasn't listening to it if he heard us knock. "Um, hi." His smile is confused at first, but grows wider as he speaks. "What is all this?"

"We wanted a late-night snack," Gretel says demurely, "and thought you might like something, too."

Noah's eyebrows knit together, like he's expecting the worst. He probably thinks Service Project and her posse of crazies are going to waltz in and give him a lap dance or something.

"We brought you Sprite!" I say, holding it up and forcing a smile. A smile that, I'm sure, looks as forced as it feels. "Or at least an all-natural, lemon-lime alternative to Sprite."

"And cookies," adds Tess.

"I do like cookies," Noah says, nudging the door so it's open all the way. "And all-natural lemon-lime alternatives." He's looking so relaxed now that I'm sure he's going to invite us in, until I remember: Noah Talbot is not the kind of guy to let girls in his room. I'm not sure if that counts as a Haven thing or a Mormon thing, but it's definitely a Noah thing.

"Noah, these are my friends Tess and Jen," I say, pointing.

"We know many things about your ways," Tess says.

Gretel and Jen both elbow her.

"What?" she asks. "We do."

"Thanks," says Noah. I'm not sure if he's thanking Tess, for her great knowledge of "his ways," or thanking us in general for the snacks, which we haven't even given him yet. But it's definitely time for us to go.

"Here." I thrust the can of Sprite-alternative at him. "Jen, give him some cookies."

"It's nice to meet you," she says, handing over the whole bag. "Really nice to meet you."

"You, too," he says, smiling again. I can only imagine

what he's really thinking. Shouldn't imagine, shouldn't care, but I still do. "Good night, Jen, Tess, Gretel, and Joy." He says each name carefully, like it's special, and he sounds like such a gentleman. But he probably rattles off the names of all the girls at school the same way. He's always a gentleman.

"Good night," I say, and it sounds a little sharper than I intend it to. "See you in the morning." I start up the stairs so everybody knows this mission is accomplished.

"Okay," Jen whispers when we reach the landing, "so if all Haven things look like that, I might be convinced to come for a visit."

ZAN HUNT

Day one of the Zan hunt dawns slightly overcast and cool, which strikes me as just the right weather to begin a day of finding someone. I imagine seeing Zan, watching the clouds part and the sun slant through as he glances up, sees me, and smiles. When he sees me, he smiles.

"I've made an appointment for us with the Pitzer admissions office," I tell Noah when I come into the kitchen. Gretel's already left for school, and her parents have already left for work. Noah's wearing a BYU T-shirt, reading the *LA Times*, and sipping (fair-trade) herb tea out of a mug Gretel made at camp. "We're taking a tour at ten. That way we can figure out the campus hot spots."

"Campus hot spots?" Noah sounds skeptical.

"Hot spots," I confirm.

It's on the tour that we're going to find Zan. I saw it in a dream.

This is how it will go. We will be walking, the tour guide and Noah and me. And the tour guide, a male whose name I do not know, is ravishingly, drop-dead, every-cliché-in-the-book handsome. And he will want me. He will be trying to make me smile, and he will be touching me in subtle not-on-purpose-but-not-by-accident ways.

And we will be stopped at a coffee cart, and he will offer to buy me a drink, and Noah will say, "A Sprite would be great, thanks," and we will ignore him. And the tour guide will have a Mocha Java and I will have a caramel steamer and over his shoulder I will see Zan. I will see Zan, and he will see me, and he will smile and time will stop and our gazes will lock and he will say, "Joy, when did you love me?"

And I will say, "Now, Zan. I love you now."

I know this. I saw it in a dream.

"And then what?" Noah says.

"And then what?" I repeat, startled. Because for a sweet, sweet split second I think about what comes next in the dream, the kiss, the kiss that will end the aching I've felt every day and every night for the last eleven weeks. The kiss that will make my body full again. The kiss that will make me full again.

But Noah's not talking about my dream. "We're taking a tour at ten and then what? What's the plan after that?"

I tear a banana off the bunch hanging from the cast-iron hook near the back window, and stare at the semi-wilted birds of paradise, their bright orange strikingly beautiful against the blue gray sky. My banana peels in perfect, even strips.

"So we're just going to take a campus tour and hope we see him along the way? *That's* the plan?"

"Noah," I say patiently, "there are currently nine hundred sixty-three students enrolled at Pitzer College. That's less than half the student body of Haven High. Statistically speaking, we're more than twice as likely to see Zan today as we are to run into him in the Haven High cafeteria."

Noah furrows his eyebrows and looks at me, with eyes that match the sky. They are not happy eyes. Finally he says: "Your ideas about statistics are questionable at best."

"Finish your tea," I tell him. "We're going to be late."

Here's how the tour really goes down. We get to Pitzer Hall early and load up on free pens and catalogs picturing ethnically diverse students. Our tour guide's name is Dave. He wears slim-cut jeans that hug his skinny legs, a faded, tight-fitting gray tee, and a hemp necklace. Likely not interested in people like me, and even if he were, not the kind of guy who'd make Zan insane with jealousy.

We're not the only ones on the tour, either. There's a guy from West Hollywood named Miguel who seems more interested in checking out the party vibe than the campus, and I can already tell I'm going to annoy him with all my questions.

"Welcome to Claremont, California," Dave says, "known as the city of trees and PhDs." He's smiling like it's supposed to be impressive, but his words make my stomach sink and crunch, sink and crunch. They remind me of that night, of Zan's angry voice yelling, "It's Oxford in the Orange Belt!"

"It's okay," Noah whispers in my ear, and I realize I've let out a so-small-you-can-hardly-hear-it scream.

GENDER-NEUTRAL HOUSING

First stop on the tour is the residence hall area, masses of buildings with student artwork painted directly on the outside walls. "Everybody has something to say," Dave tells us. "The administration respects that."

It seems to me like something maybe the administration shouldn't respect quite so much, because most of the "graffiti art" looks heavy on the graffiti and light on the art, at least to my eyes. But Zan lives within these walls, somewhere. These are Zan's walls, and they can look however they want to look, because he is inside.

"Another thing the administration respects is the individual's right to decide with whom he or she will cohabitate." He knocks on one of the dorm doors and a girl yells for us to come in.

"Decide with whom he or she will cohabitate?" asks Noah.

I shrug. "No idea. Roommate selection, maybe?"

The room we walk into is just a few feet by another few feet. Our hostess is nodding along to her iPod while lying on her bed, which is so close to the ceiling she can't even sit up without hitting her head. Under her bed is her desk, covered with stuff, and her dresser, also covered with stuff. The other side of the room is identical.

Glass bottles line the windowsill, and the air is thick, stale-beer air. I haven't smelled stale-beer air in so long, and I don't think Noah has *ever* smelled stale-beer air because his face is contorted like he's trying not to breathe. The vein beneath his eye twitches.

Dave is, out of necessity, standing too close to me. I breathe in patchouli and male body odor, which, coupled with the stale-beer air, makes me woozy. As I move closer to Noah my foot ends up sliding on something, and I sort of fall onto him. I look down at the satiny panties now spread across Noah's white sneaker. To his credit, Noah doesn't say anything or even attempt to move. He just steadies me and tries to smile.

The girl who lives here is willing to show *this* off?

"Cornelia's chosen to room with another female this semester," Dave says as Cornelia resumes staring at the ceiling. "They share the bathroom"—he motions to the door behind me, which I don't dare try to open—"with a male/female room, making this a single-sex room, coed suite. Anyone can live with whomever they want to. We're the first campus in the country with one-hundred-percent gender-neutral housing."

Gender-neutral housing.

I think about these walls, Zan's walls, and I can see myself living with him. Our place would be nothing like this place, with disgusting smells and underwear on the floor. Our place would be organized courtesy of IKEA. We'd have cool bumper stickers and a poster of Noam Chomsky on the wall, and the bottles on the windowsill would be filled with fresh flowers. After class Zan would come in, set his books on the desk, and ask me how my day was and did I want to get something to eat? And we'd have all our meals together and at night he'd tuck me in and lie next to me until I fell asleep, then sleep in his own bed because, even with gender-neutral housing, there are limits.

Limits. And I'm back to reality; back to knowing there's no way this gender-neutral concept would fly with my parents, or my religion, or even with me. But the dream of it all. I can't help savoring the last, forbidden sweetness of the dream of it all.

It's about this time that I start needing some air and I think everybody else does, too, because Dave says it's time to move on.

HOT SPOT

Outside, a eucalyptus tree bows overhead, its creamy-colored bark like elephant's skin, smooth and taut over some bumps, loose and sagging over others. Zan's here, somewhere. Somewhere, Zan's here.

Noah follows my gaze. "Looks like an elephant," he says casually, pointing. I don't want him to be the one saying it. I want Zan to be the one saying it, Zan to be the one reading my mind.

"What's wrong?" Noah asks me, and there's the concern in his voice I haven't heard this whole trip—not since Homecoming night at my house. "You look pale."

"I always look pale," I say, swallowing hard. "I am pale." Which is true. I am. But I still feel the nonexistent color draining from my face. What's wrong with me? We're here. We're one step closer to finding Zan. And I'm not scared. I'm not nervous. But I'm not happy. I don't know what I am. "Anyway, I'm fine," I say, which is not for sure true but definitely the right thing to say, because Noah nods and his shoulders relax.

"Okay," says Dave, "let's check out the campus hot spot, shall we?"

"Did he just say 'campus hot spot'?" I whisper to Noah. My practically nonexistent arm hair is standing straight up on my practically colorless arms.

Noah at least pretends not to notice the coincidence. *"Did he just say 'shall we'?"* he whispers back.

"We have our own coffeehouse here." Dave walks backward while facing us, and I wonder how tour guides learn to do that without bumping into things. "It's a restored Craftsman-style cottage the college bought back in the 1950s and moved to right . . ."

He slows then stops. "Here. Ballad of the Sad Café. Best coffee in the Los Angeles County area, and *the* place for on-campus happenings. Student art exhibits upstairs, student recitals downstairs. The improv group performs here, the garage bands play here, student filmmakers have screenings here. This is the place to see and be seen."

The place to see and be seen.

That's exactly what I want.

To see and be seen.

I don't pay attention to the rest of the tour.

We go through buildings and talk about study abroad and are told dates and statistics, but I don't care. Zan is as good as found.

So we finish back where we started.

Noah's being all polite, telling Dave thanks and Miguel it was nice to meet him, but I'm still in a daze. Zan is as good as found.

"So, whatdya think?" Noah's eyes are deep blue and excited. "Lunchtime?"

I nod. "Let's go."

THE BALLAD

"So," says Noah. "Ballad of the Sad Café. We meet again."

We're not really meeting again—the two-second walk-through on the tour barely qualifies as an introduction. My stomach drops, even though this is just a coffee shop. But it's more than a coffee shop, really. It's like my whole future is in here, waiting for me to live it. My past and my future, melding into one. This is how it should be.

"Doesn't it smell good?" I inhale deeply as I push open the door. There's this robust and somehow comforting aroma permeating the place. Right off I can tell Zan loves it here.

On one table a chess game is waiting to be played. New Age music is blaring through the speakers and there's real art on the walls. There are a few old diner-style booths around the room, and there's a group of students at one, looking deep in conversation. I am vaguely aware of Noah, hands in pockets, whistling.

"Will you cut it out? You're embarrassing me."

"What?" He goes back to whistling "On Top of Old Smokey." Idiot.

This place is full of memories. I long to have them become my memories. I want to live this life, too. But more than that, I want to have already lived this life. I want for Zan and me to have lived it together.

That smell again. Nowhere in Haven smells like this. We're probably the only town in America not to have a Starbucks, and Phil's Market doesn't even sell fresh coffee beans. I drink in the air, swallow the smell. "I bet Zan has breakfast here every morning."

Noah's gaze is fixed on the ceiling and he sniffs the air warily. "What makes you say that?"

"He liked Mocha Java," I say, calming myself with another inhale-exhale routine. "Right before he left. He started drinking Mocha Java. I was worried, about him drinking coffee. I worried that this was something way bigger than just hating Haven—this was hating the Church. But I don't worry for him anymore. He's just moved on. Now he's here, drinking Mocha Java and eating bagels."

"Well, technically he's not *here* here." Noah looks at the few groups sprinkled throughout the room. It's only eleven fifteen, I realize, glancing at the old-school wall clock. No college spot, however hot, is happening at eleven fifteen in the morning.

Noah wanders over to the huge bulletin board on the east wall, but Zan consumes me so much I feel too heavy to move. He's here. And maybe our values are a little different now, but that doesn't matter. We can have different values and still be the same. We're still the same. Joyand-Zan. ZanandJoy.

Noah's silent a moment. "Did you know that the amount of money the U.S. spends on weapons in a week is enough to feed the whole world for a year? A whole year." He stares at a flyer that says FOOD NOT BOMBS tacked up next to an advertisement for yoga classes.

"Noah, have you been listening to me?"

He sighs. "Yes, and I have to tell you that your idea of closure is, in my humble opinion, a little bit skewed."

"Meaning?"

"Meaning, what if he's moved on in more ways than just being able to get a decent cup of coffee? What if he's moved on because he's actually moved on? We, meanwhile, have moved backward. *You've* moved backward!"

Noah's upset now, so I'm upset, too. I can't stay calm when he's not. I can't stay calm most of the time, but I *definitely* can't when he can't.

"Shut up! Who are you to talk about moving on? You're here, too. It wasn't just me who wanted to pack up and head to California."

He could argue this point, but he doesn't. He clenches and unclenches his fists a few times, which seems to purge the freak energy.

"Listen, I don't blame you for wanting closure. That's fine. I want it, too. But I can't let you parade around this place like it's Graceland and Zan's Elvis. I know you better than that. I know you're above this stalking business."

"What do you suggest we do, then?"

"We do what we both know you came here to do. We meet up with Zan. We see if he's the Zan you remember. The Zan you want to be with."

I pretend to be engrossed in a piece of art on the wall until I notice the title is *Naked Woman: Distorted*. I look up at Noah. His eyes are so clear I can only stare into them for a minute without getting dizzy.

"Joy." Noah's voice is quiet. "Will you promise me one thing?" He lowers his head. "I know you remember Zan a certain way. But if we find Zan and he doesn't match up with the memories . . . the Zanories"—Noah smiles, tiny—"then let him go, okay? I can't stand to see you get hurt again."

KIRCHENDORF

I need to put one hand over each of my temples and squeeze in as hard as I can. That is what I need to do. It's the only way to get rid of this feeling. But I can't. So I sit down instead. I sit down on a paisley-upholstered chair and say: "Whatever."

Noah swallows, and I can physically see him losing the melodrama of a moment ago. "Let's still get lunch while we're here, okay?"

I stand up, slowly. The floor seems solid enough, so I nod. "Yeah, okay."

We walk up to the front counter and out of nowhere a new crop of students crowds in behind us. I like the misguided feeling that we started a trend. The daily specials, scrawled in pink chalk, are impossible to read.

"I'm asking the next person I talk to if he knows Zan," says Noah.

"Don't you dare." I keep my voice low. "That's about a hundred times more stalkerish than anything I've done this entire trip."

"It's about a hundred times more *sensible* than any-thing you've done this entire trip," Noah says to me. To the shaggy-haired kid behind the counter he says, "I'll have a four cheese quesadilla, please. You?" Noah nods at me.

I haven't had a chance to look at the menu. "The daily special."

The kid looks confused. "Which one?"

I shrug. "I don't know. The top one."

"Turkey with avocado on seven grain?"

I nod, and he's ringing up the total when Noah really does ask, "By the way, do you know Alexander Kirchen-dorf?"

By the way? Oh, casually and by the way, do you know some random student? I can't believe he's doing this to me.

The shaggy-haired kid behind the counter shakes his head. "Nope." He pauses. "Hey, Justine?" he yells over the music to a girl filling a blue ceramic mug. "Do you know an Alexander Kirchendorf?"

And it's like one of those movie moments when every-thing freezes. There's a split-second pause while the ste-reo switches songs, a million conversations lull, and the refrigerator stops humming. It's dead silent while Justine says: "Wait, Kirchendorf?" She pauses between syllables, making it sound even longer. "Kirchendorf, like German? For church?"

Like German for church. For church. Everything comes back to that, doesn't it? Back to the church he doesn't believe in. Back to the church that was so much a part of him it's still his name.

Then Justine's standing in front of me, her curly black hair falling out of its sloppy bun, her black eyes looking earnest. She's holding out a sheet of paper. "I don't know him," she says. "But is this the guy you're looking for?"

There's a list of names scrawled across the paper. Larger than the rest is one name in familiar handwriting, a crazy-beautiful hybrid of lowercase and caps.

Kirchendorf.

"I'm writing my thesis on the historical significance of surnames," Justine tells me. My eyes are still drawn to his name, his handwriting. "Your friend's name popped out at me. In fact, if he'd be up for an interview . . ."

"What's this list for?" I interrupt her.

She points to the heading, and both Noah and I look closer. "Open-mike poetry reading," she says. "Tonight."

Open-mike poetry night. Noah and I share a look. Of course.

Not that Zan read poetry at open-mike night back

home. "Bunch of no-talent wannabes," he said about the poetry club at Haven High. Harsh, but true. "When I give a reading it'll be with *real* writers."

Now he's found them. Tonight at eight o'clock he'll be with real writers and I'll be with him.

SLEEPING ON IT

We finish eating, and once we get outside, the sun is already beginning to peek through the clouds. I can tell Noah's pleased, but not because of the weather—because he's the kind of guy who really, really likes to have a plan. "Okay," he says, checking his phone. "So, we know what we're doing tonight. What's next on our agenda?"

I say it before I can think not to. "Sleep?" The Zan hunt's been more exhausting than I'd anticipated, and the seven-grain sandwich sits heavy in my stomach and fuzzy on my mind.

Everywhere kids are sprawled out studying under trees, and there's a breeze, and all I want to do is sprawl out, or curl up, anything where I don't have to think or speak or move. "Let's go back to Gretel's."

Noah nods.

I lead him in a windy detour that will take us back to our car via the Scripps campus. Elm trees dot the lawn, and their pattern reminds me of argyle socks. "Scripps always makes me feel like I'm in an Impressionist painting," I tell Noah, kicking a golden leaf off the walkway.

"It's . . . prettier here, isn't it?" he says. It's unexpected, how he says it, that he says it at all.

I nod. "It's the prettiest place in the world, as far as I'm concerned." It's almost too beautiful. Seeing all the girls walk past me—smart, driven, focused girls with a purpose—it's more than I can take. That my purpose here is to find my boyfriend has never felt more pathetic.

I spot a nice empty space under a tree just down the road. It's away from the smart girls, and it's a place I can rest without being reminded of everything I should be doing: how I should be better than this, how I should have found Zan already, how I shouldn't even need to be finding him at all. How I should be a competent, confident young woman who doesn't need a man—and men want her all the more because of it. That's who I should be. I have to get away from the shoulds.

"Let's go there," I say, pointing. "I'm too tired to get all the way to the car without stopping first. Is that okay?"

"Sure it is," says Noah, surprised. "Whatever you want."

I take out my denim jacket and spread it over my backpack. Noah sits with his back against the tree's massive trunk.

"I used to want to go to college here," I say, resting my head against my jacket/backpack pillow.

"But not anymore?" Noah says.

I close my eyes. The air feels perfect here. At home, it's already starting to get too cold. "Now I don't know with . . . everything going on. I don't know where the right place is for me."

"You'll figure it out," Noah says, and I yawn.

"I hope so."

ULTIMATE

𝓣𝓱𝓮 𝓷𝓮𝔁𝓽 𝓽𝓱𝓲𝓷𝓰 I hear is a voice. A loud one.

"You've gotta move, man. We need to practice."

"Practice playing Frisbee?" I recognize this voice. It's Noah's. I can't bring myself to open my eyes.

"No, not Frisbee. *Ultimate*. It's the off-season, but we've got to stay in shape. And this is where we practice. So wake up your girlfriend and move." This voice is deeper than the first, but also more annoying.

I know at this point I should fully wake up, open my eyes, and tell these guys to quit making stupid assumptions. That I'm not Noah's girlfriend, but that if they ask nicely we'll leave.

Before I can bring myself to move, though, Noah starts talking. Of course. He'll set the record straight. I'm *not* his girlfriend. We'll just move. It's no big deal.

I think I'm asleep still, dreaming, when he says: "Can't you just let her sleep? We're not really in your way." How he says it, though, it sounds like: "You *will* let her sleep, and you *will* leave us the hell alone." I mean, if a guy like Noah Talbot said things like "leave us the hell alone."

It's the first time I've heard Noah opt for confrontation. He's opting for confrontation and he's opting for it because of me. That's how I know this is real—my subconscious wouldn't even know how to make this up. No guy's ever opted for confrontation because of me before, let alone the calmest guy I've ever met. I can't help that it makes my insides tingle a little.

"The sun's too bright over here anyway," the annoying voice says, and I hear two sets of footsteps tromp off.

I yawn, stretch, and then slowly open my eyes. "Hey." I shift so that I'm sitting next to him.

"Hey," says Noah, looking over at me. "How'd you sleep?"

I shoot him a thumbs-up. It's cozy, under the shade tree, relaxing with Noah. Too cozy. My mind is still in a comfortable haze until I all-the-way wake up and realize how wrong everything in my life is.

"Let's go," I say, hopping up so quickly that Noah looks startled.

"Okay," he says. "You still want to go back?" He looks all expectant, eager-to-please, and I know now's the time I could ask him to go on a tour of every public restroom in the vicinity and he'd do it, no questions asked. That's just the kind of guy he is, and this is just the moment he's being himself the most.

But I still want to go home. This day already feels like it's been eighty hours long. And I need my energy for tonight. When I tell this to Noah, he looks relieved, but all he says is, "Your wish is my command."

We cross the street to head back to the SAAB, strolling a little because I'm still sort of sleepy and it's a beautiful day, really. All the buildings glisten. They are at their most beautiful, ready to be photographed for brochures and course catalogues.

"Oh, good, we were just about to start!" A girl comes bounding out of the building we're passing. She's an obvious dancer, with long, gangly-tree limbs, good posture, and the kind of wavy hair that falls effortlessly into a messy-but-not-really bun.

She holds one of the glass doors open for us. "I'm glad you guys showed up. It's always good to have a few 'real people' in the audience for dress rehearsal, you know?"

Noah and I exchange a glance, and in that glance we both realize what we've been roped into. This is a dance recital, and there's no way we can leave now without looking like jerks. And we aren't jerks. Especially not Noah.

"Real people are good," Noah agrees, nodding. To someone else it would look like a typical nod, but I feel Noah's resignation to his fate with every bob of his head.

The girl laughs, even though nothing's funny. "We're having problems with the lighting," she says, leading us to a small theater. "Let us know what you think after the performance, okay?'

There's seating for maybe fifty people, on uncomfortable-looking chairs, mostly occupied by other dance types. The stage is a plain white dance floor, with a remote-controlled car skittering all over it.

"Very postmodern," Noah says, seriously, as we find seats near the exit.

"Oh, like you have any idea."

"Whatever. I'm Lord of the Dance." Noah says this last part in a whisper, raising his eyebrows.

"I happen to know this to be false," I say. "You've told me you don't like dancing. Twice."

My knowing this makes him happier, because when he looks at me he smiles. "Wow, you remember. Impressive."

"Then you're easily impressed," I say, smiling back. I shift in my chair, which feels as awkward as it looks. I wonder how long this is going to be.

Just then the lights dim, a single beam illuminating a section of the stage.

"And we're off," Noah says.

UNDRESSED REHEARSAL

A dancer walks onto the stage. She's not in the leotard/toe shoes getup I expect to see. She's in . . . well, practically nothing. The two pieces she wears are skimpier than short-shorts and a tank top but significantly less hot than a bikini. It's more like she's wearing underwear—drab, unflattering underwear.

Overhead, a voice describes the dancer. It booms like the voice of God: Asian-American. One hundred and fifteen pounds. Emotionally fragile.

The girl just stands there, and I think, "Hey, even *I* could do this kind of dance."

She steps aside, and a male dancer takes the stage. He's wearing a drab, Speedo-looking thing that blends into his gingerbread-colored skin. If he was more attractive I would look away. He isn't, so I just stare at him as the narrator calls him: Small-boned. Homosexual. Easily frightened.

More dancers take the stage in various states of near-

nakedness, each of them described as they stand, illumi-
nated.

"Um, so, is this the dance?" Noah whispers into my ear.

"Maybe?" I whisper back. *"I'm not sure. I'm not really
into dance."*

Slowly, colored lights flutter across the stage, casting
long, distorted shadows on the wall. So far, the lighting
is my favorite part of the show. I make a mental note to
tell bun-girl.

Then, the dancing. Bodies contort, flat stomachs
moving with labored breath, gangly tree limbs swaying
against time with the tuneless music now blaring through
the speakers. Some spin while others stand. Others stand
while some spin. The bodies are beautiful to watch, I admit—but it's a tricky thing, watching bodies that are between seventy-six and eighty percent unclothed.

Especially while sitting next to the angelic Noah Talbot, who's slumping in his seat uncomfortably. I'd have
more fun watching him squirm if I wasn't enjoying myself
so little. The dancers seem to be in pain, and I flinch with
each gasp they take, so I move my stare to the walls. The
shadows flit and sway like my thoughts, jumping from
one idea to another, bending before I can finish thinking
them through.

The dance doesn't end. The dancers struggle for breath

and mimic dying so many times I realize death won't signal a stop. Maybe that's the point—maybe "dead" is just another label I'm willing to throw on these people, the same as I would label someone a vegan. Gray-eyed. Dead.

My inability to open my mind frustrates me. All I can think about is Zan. Caucasian. Facial-haired. Loved by Joy.

Finally, the lights come on before I realize the dance is ending. The harshness of the bright overheads overwhelms me.

The girl in the bun rushes over to me. "So what'd you think?"

"The lighting was great!" I say too quickly, with too much enthusiasm.

She nods and plies off to another group.

Noah gives me a helpless look. "Can we go home now?"

I nod. "Yes, please."

MY OUTFIT FOR
OPEN-MIKE NIGHT

Wide-leg jeans
Tissue-weight ribbed black top
   (long sleeved)
Gold satin ballet flats
Raspberry lip gloss

NOAH'S OUTFIT FOR OPEN-MIKE NIGHT

Bootcut khakis

Maroon tee

Denim jacket

(No Senior Discount hat)

GO TIME

𝕴𝖙'𝖘 𝕱𝖗𝖎𝖉𝖆𝖞 𝖓𝖎𝖌𝖍𝖙 at Ballad of the Sad Café, and the air smells like melodrama and espresso. The place is packed with girls wearing Scripps College hoodies and guys with too much facial hair. Noah asks for Sprite, of course, and I get hot chocolate. I've seen how much whipped cream they put on top and then sprinkle with cocoa powder.

There's a hand-lettered sign telling us the poetry reading is downstairs, so I'm holding my hot chocolate mug very carefully as we go down a circular staircase. "Let me take that," says Noah, and he does, and he carries both drinks and he doesn't spill a single drop and I could never be like that. I could never carry two drinks without spilling like the perfect Noah Talbot.

The whole upstairs of the Ballad is funky-chic Craftsman-style, with these great old light fixtures and cool moldings. But the downstairs is stuck in a much less sought-after era. The tables are made of scratched, avocado-colored Formica. The light fixtures aren't "great

187

old," they're seventies old, made of brass with burned-out bulbs—dim enough so that you almost don't see the green shag rug. Almost.

"Let's sit here," I say, and we sit at a table in the back corner, where we can see everyone come in but, because of the shadows, they can't see us.

A guy in a newsboy hat and an oversize tweed jacket is adjusting the microphone up front. We're early, so the room is still pretty empty, but I do see one girl who's obviously been here a while, because when she walks in carrying a string of lights she says to Newsboy Hat: "Found them!" At first I think she's going to hang them, and apparently, so does she. Noticing nowhere to hang them from, she finally decides to wrap them in a big circle beneath the microphone.

"I need a refill," Noah says, standing up.

"Already?"

He holds up his empty glass as proof, and I realize that while I've been staring, taking it all in, he's been drinking, more literally taking it all in. "You want anything?" he asks.

I haven't touched my hot chocolate yet. "No, I'm good."

Noah takes off, and I see the girl look up; she hadn't noticed we were in the room until now. She gazes into the corner, then steps off the "stage" and comes over to me.

"Hey," she says. "I'm Lizzy." Lizzy's wearing a wrap-around miniskirt and a shirt with a brown stain on the shoulder. "That's Preston." She motions at Newsboy Hat. "We're co-presidents of the Poetry Society."

"Hi." I try to smile, but not too big, not a fakey-fake Haven smile. "Nice to meet you."

Lizzy waits two beats. "And you are?" she prompts.

"Oh, I'm . . . I'm Joy." I fumble. "And my . . . friend, that's Noah who just went upstairs."

"Cool. You guys freshmen?"

"We're on a college visit, actually. Checking out the campus."

Her eyes light up. "Seriously? I give campus tours."

"We took a tour today. Guy named Dave." I look at her and she nods. She either knows him or is willing to pretend like she does.

"What did you think of Pitzer?" she asks, excitedly. So excitedly that she doesn't wait for my response. "It's great isn't it? I love this place. It should totally make your short list."

It embarrasses me to admit, even to myself, that I don't yet have (nor am I even formulating) a short list. No way I'll admit it to her. So why did admitting it to Mr. Daniel, College Counselor De-strodinaire, not embarrass me at all?

"So, you're into poetry?" Lizzy looks genuinely interested. I wonder if it's a look she's had to acquire as a tour guide—feigning interest in potential recruits—or if she really is, for whatever reason, interested in what my hobbies are.

I think about poetry, about the poems Zan used to write me in Estar. "Yeah."

Lizzy smiles. "Excellent."

Noah comes down the stairs and Lizzy says, "You must be Noah," and we make introductions and it hits me. We're actually here. This is actually all real.

Something in the front of the room falls, or at least there's a crash. It startles all three of us. "I'd better go help Preston," Lizzy says sheepishly. "Nice meeting you."

"Ditto," says Noah. Anyone else saying that—*ditto*—and it would sound stupid to the extreme, but with Noah's natural ease and friendliness around people, it just sounds right.

As we've been talking to Lizzy, the room has slowly been filling, and I've been scoping it out. No Zan, of course, but there's a decent showing. And even though it shouldn't matter, I notice that Noah is by far the best-looking guy here. He's not overly clean-cut or preppy, either—he doesn't stand out in a pretty boy way.

His all-the-right-shades of sandy blond hair falls in his face. I love how his hair's grown out just slightly long—long enough to look hip but not mangy, like so many of the guys here. Somehow his eyes look bluer in the lack of light. Not an ounce of him looks out of place.

Meanwhile, I'm guessing that *every* ounce of me looks out of place, as out of place as I feel, but I don't care. This is the kind of out-of-place feeling I love; the kind of out-of-place feeling that makes me tingly all over and numb from my shoulders down to my elbows. This is not my uncomfortable brand of out-of-placeness. This is the out-of-placeness I thrive on. The out-of-placeness I felt with Zan.

Zan. I still haven't seen him. I've seen a girl in fish-net stockings, embroidered with a rose pattern winding down the leg. I've seen a guy in the world's largest pair of glasses. I've seen a token old lady, gray-haired and over-weight. I've seen a black dachshund wandering around, in what is surely a violation of the health code. I have not seen Zan.

Everybody has their own book with them—a brown leather journal seems to be standard issue. I can't help thinking of purple velvet, and then not knowing what to think.

Maybe that's why it feels so out of place when Noah puts his hand on my hand. Maybe that's why my skin heats up to three hundred degrees in record time. Or maybe it's because I'm psychic, and I already know what he's going to say, which is, "Heads-up, Joy. Look who just walked in."

IN THE FLESH

Recognition comes to me in bits and pieces. Dark hair, shiny like Zan's, only longer. Goatee like Zan's, only thicker. Brown eyes like Zan's, only darker. True, he's wearing cutoff cargos (he never wears shorts) and a slightly too-tight shirt with orange sleeves and the words GRAND CANYON on the front, but it's definitely him. My heart doesn't finish beating before another beat begins. I've found him. I've found him.

Then I see someone following, winding down the circular stairs holding onto his hand. Right then I want to jump up and save Zan from whoever this is, whoever is leeching onto his hand, because doesn't she know Zan doesn't hold hands? Why would she do that? Why would he let her?

She has hair halfway down her back, and it's the color of a million shades of sunrise. A row of shiny studs curve around her ear, and her white halter hugs her body and reveals broad, tanned shoulders. She's wearing a pair of those shorts with the half-inch inseam.

I'm not jealous, but I still remember how I've never been able to grow my hair past my shoulders, how I never pierced my ears even once because I fear fainting, how I never wear halter tops or spaghetti straps.

"Why is she holding his hand?" I ask Noah.

Noah just looks at me, and his eyes hurt. His hand is still on top of mine but ice-blood has cooled my skin to a chilly negative-one-hundred-degrees. Squared.

BEATDICK

He doesn't see me. And part of me knows I'm in the corner where he can't see me, that I've chosen to sit where I can observe without being observed. But that common-sense part of me is long gone by now, and all I can think is, *Why doesn't he see me?*

I watch him sit down with the girl, at a table near the front, and I look at Noah and open my mouth but no words are there. He nods, though, and his hand is still on my hand, and he lifts me up and we move to a closer table.

There are already two other people there, girls in berets, but they just smile like it's cool, mainly smiling at Noah, I think, but I can't tell because my eyes are on Zan. I don't want him to see me, but I do want him to see me, and I want both those things so much and why doesn't he see me?

Lights shine blue against the green carpet and Preston and Lizzy are at the mike, welcoming everyone to the first poetry reading of the year. There's clapping and thankfully no snapping, and everybody seems nice enough except the skanky girl still clutching Zan's hand. Her breasts ride up a little too close to Zan's face as she whispers something to him. I know I'm staring, and on one hand I know that's tacky, but on the other hand I think about how Zan's not looking at me, and it hurts triple-time because why doesn't he see me?

Everybody starts with their poems and I might hear one or I might hear twenty, but it's just one long stream of words I don't understand or even want to understand. And I think I might be crying but I can't even tell anymore, because my body and I haven't been on speaking terms for awhile now.

Until something halfway wakes me up.

He stands in the circle of blue lights, standing there like that circle on that shag carpet belongs to him. He's so sure of himself, like always, but this time it doesn't look right. Now he's here, with his people, the people we were never as good as, but he still looks like he's better than we are. Or is it just that he *thinks* he's better than we are? I can't tell.

Seeing his bare legs for the first time, covered in so much thick, black hair, nauseates me. I never thought about what Zan's legs looked like. He never showed them to me, to anyone, as far as I knew. Here he is, exposed, but he's still wearing that same smirk that used to irritate Mattia beyond belief.

Then I see it. I see it and I swallow the scream because he's wearing flip-flops. I've never seen Zan wear flip-flops. I've never seen him wear any shoes besides his signature brown loafers. Even in the middle of summer, he wore his loafers. Zan without his loafers—it's like he's left behind who he was.

Who he was with me.

ZAN'S POEM

I saw the best minds of my generation wasted
By conformity, dreams fading to black and
White. Cutouts
Dragging themselves through the pristine streets
  of a cardboard town looking for a
Savior
There was a cardboard girl there, in the
  cardboard world, but I felt no connection
Even tearing down the walls
Each shard breathed promise they'd never know
They cry stagnant, hollow tears.

REACTION SHOT

𝐼 can't finish thinking a thought, because each one gets interrupted midway through. But I do hear Noah mutter something I've never heard him say before: "That guy is truly an A-hole."

While the next poet gets up, Noah borrows a pen from one of the bereted girls, takes the napkin from underneath his drink, and starts scribbling furiously.

All around me there are words, being scribbled, being shouted, being elongated for rhythm. There are so many words, but no words for what I'm feeling, for what I'm seeing.

Then Noah picks up his napkin and stands, walking over to Lizzy and whispering something in her ear. She gets up and straightens her miniskirt, which has slid halfway around her waist. Everyone is looking at our table, and the bereted girls shrug, and I see Zan, and finally he sees me, and his eyes register nothing. He turns back around.

"We're pleased to welcome two potential Pitzer students here with us tonight," Lizzy says, smiling. "Joy and Noah are visiting the campus and wanted to check out the poetry scene here. Turns out Noah's a poet, too, so we're going to slightly amend our program to let him share his work." She smiles again, then nods to him.

I have the first clear thought that I have all day: This cannot be good.

NOAH'S POEM

You're one of those people
Who don't know what you have until it's gone
And sometimes not even then
Because look, man, she's right in front of you
Look, Zan, she's right in front of you

You said keep an eye on her
Meaning keep her away
So stupid, thought it'd be easy
I didn't see her devotion to you
Until I saw how it wasn't for me
Because look, man, she's right in front of you
Look, Zan, she's right in front of you.

Her green-gray eyes
They're for you
Her secret smile
That, too

Idiot, she calls me
And I wish she knew
I might be an idiot
But you're an idiot, too
Because look, man, she's right in front of you
Look, Zan, she's right in front of you.

REACTION SHOT

By the time the clapping-thankfully-not-snapping dies down, and by the time Noah gets back to the table, I think I must be crying or maybe something like it, because he says, "Want to get out of here?" and I say, "Yes, please."

DREAM COME TRUE

We're upstairs, but not out the door yet, when I hear someone yell, "What the hell was that?" and I know it's Zan.

The Ballad's busy, busy enough that no one really notices or cares about the yelling, busy enough that Zan has to wedge his way between a bunch of people to get to us, black-and-tan coffee cup in hand. I see the blonde skank right behind him, holding a mug with the string from her tea bag draped over the side. It's odd to me how they were in such a hurry to find us, but still brought their cups along, like we were really just getting together for drinks.

I don't know who Zan's yell was actually directed at. It might have been me. These might be the first words he says to me after all this time. This, all this, might actually be my dream come true.

Noah doesn't stop walking, out the quaint double doors, into the sweet-smelling, still-warm, perfect-black night. I feel like I'm trapped in a fairy tale.

Zan and the girl follow, too, and now we're alone. There are lights all around us, of course, from buildings and streetlights and windows, but the darkness still makes me feel that we're even more alone: that we four are the only people on the planet right now.

Zan kind of gets up into Noah's face, but it's not very menacing because when they stand side by side, it's obvious how much taller and bigger Noah is. I didn't realize it until now. "So? What the hell is going on?"

"Dude, step back," says Noah calmly, lightly pushing Zan away. "Isn't it obvious? We came here supposedly on a college visit, but mainly to find you. Joy needed to see you."

"You needed to see him, too," I say. Great. The first time I can manage to open my mouth, and I'm talking to Noah, not Zan. "I mean, we both needed to see you. To . . ." Telling the truth seems pathetic now, with this half-naked Bohemian princess hugging Zan's waist like she owns him. "We needed to get closure," I say, and for the first time the lie sounds like the truth.

"Closure? What, were you his *girlfriend* or something?" The girl stretches out the word "girlfriend" so it sounds all second grade. She smiles and yeah, it's a gorgeous smile. Her teeth glisten, probably naturally even and white.

My teeth look like salt-and-pepper corn in comparison, but I smile, too. I match her tone, two parts condescending, one part pitying. "I still am his girlfriend or something. Why, didn't he tell you about me?" I was all pumped to be sad. In fact, in the Ballad I'm pretty sure I was crying. But now I'm feeling an emotion best described by words I would never actually say: I am pissed off.

"You are *not* my girlfriend," says Zan, and he definitely sounds second grade, so he changes his tone to one I'm more familiar with. "I don't have a girlfriend."

Noah raises his eyebrows. "Oh, really?" Noah looks at the girl, pointedly.

"Ismene is not my girlfriend," Zan says coolly. Her name sounds like "ease-men," which, judging from Zan's expression, she certainly seems to do. "We're simply in a relationship."

I can't stand to look at them, any of them. I stare down to look at nothing, but beneath the window's glow I end up seeing Zan's feet. Zan's feet, in blue flip-flops. They're probably made from organic plastic or something else socially-conscious, but they look like shoes you could buy for three dollars at Old Navy.

I've never seen his toes, and they are especially ugly. They're too hairy, too long, and the nails are thick and yellowing at the corners. If I had toes like that, I'd keep them covered all the time. If I had toes like that, I wouldn't—

"We don't believe in labels," Ismene says. Because of that stupid window light I can see she is wearing blue mascara. *Why do they always wear blue mascara?* "Alex and I believe in complete emotional freedom."

I have no idea what the "complete emotional freedom" garbage she's spouting is all about, but it seems completely irrelevant. "Who's Alex?" Noah and I ask at the same time.

Ismene laughs. As much as I wish her laugh were an overloud, oversnorty, cringe-worthy sound, it isn't. It's a light, gentle laugh—a laugh you want to join in even if you don't know what's funny, just so that laugh is with you, not at you. Her grip around Zan's waist tightens. "These people were your *friends*, Alex? No wonder you never talk about them."

Zan is Alex. Zan is Alex who wears shorts and flip-flops and takes his Mocha Java with him everywhere he goes and writes condescending, lame rip-off beat poetry and has ugly toes. Alex is Zan, who once wore his grandpa's loafers and didn't believe in drinking coffee because he was Mormon and wrote me love poetry in Estar and I wasn't cardboard, not then, not back when he was Zan. Back when he was easier to love.

Now he never talks about me.

Alex/Zan snuggles closer to Ismene. "Didn't you ever

wonder why there aren't any pictures of my high school friends in our room?"

Now he never talks about me and doesn't keep any pictures of me in their room. In their room. And suddenly I'm thinking gender-neutral housing, and suddenly I can't breathe again, and suddenly my heart starts pumping and Oh. My.

If this were a teen movie, the camera would be shaking right now. Then, the reaction shots. First my face. Zan's. Noah's. Hers. In each frame, realization would cross our faces. Noah would see what I knew. Zan would see what Noah and I both knew. The girl would be clueless still, perhaps as a form of comic relief.

But this is not a teen movie. I never wanted to be part of a teen movie. I wanted this to be my dream-come-true. I know now that test at Mattia's wasn't out of a hundred—it was out of ninety-six. Dreams don't predict diddly-squat. Dreams lead you astray.

Follow dreams and you find yourself beaten down, torn between being mocked and being ignored. This boy I once loved is living with a girl. He's living with a girl who wears halter tops and lots of earrings and is not me. He's in a relationship with a girl and she's living with him, and she's not me and Oh. My.

I've never wished harder for tea to stain teeth.

I'm done with this, all this, this dream-come-true adventure in "closure." I'm out.

I look up at Alex/Zan, into the eyes I once loved, and I tell him, "You have the most hideous toes I have ever seen."

THE AFTERMATH

And I run. And I'm not a very graceful runner, or a very fast runner, or even a very good runner, and it shows because before long I am panting, completely out of breath, and I haven't even made it that far. Noah's caught up with me, easily, and as I'm heaving, and as my lungs are collapsing, Noah's right next to me breathing all naturally, the way normal people breathe.

Perfect Noah, who didn't even want to come here in the first place, who got dragged along by a crazy girl because he was trying to do the Right Thing. He was trying to fix things and now he's stuck here, with this girl going into cardiac arrest because she apparently has the body of a seventy-five-year-old asthmatic.

We just walk. We just go slow and wait while I get my breath back and we just walk and I think about how nothing is turning out like it's supposed to turn out and I'm just some person walking and not knowing where I'm going. There is no difference between me and any other lonely person in this world.

I know these streets. These are the streets of my child-
hood, where the homes have character and gardens and
big old trees. You can walk anywhere worth going in this
city, and I walk. I walk so long I forget that Noah is right
next to me. Noah's steps have blended into mine and we
walk.

HISTORY LESSON

Finally Noah says: "Do you know where we are? Because I don't."

"I know where we are," I say. "This is the neighborhood where I grew up."

Noah starts talking again before I want him to. "You have a lot of history here."

I nod, but the only history I can think of is what just went down with Zan. For the moment, it's the only history worth remembering. "It doesn't make any sense. When I was here, I didn't have him. When I wasn't here, I did have him. Now I'm here and he's here and I should have everything, but I don't."

It isn't right that the air should feel so good tonight, so soft and comfortable. I know exactly what tonight should feel like: smothering air thick with southern California smog. Air you go inside to avoid breathing. We get that kind of air here, sometimes. We should have it tonight, but of course we don't. Of course tonight is perfect. "Maybe this puts everything in perspective."

"Like what?"

"How I don't have anything. How I don't have him and I don't have my home and I don't have my history. How I'm going to leave here with nothing just like I did last time. Only this time it's so much worse. This time I know what's waiting for me."

I'm crying and I don't care. "I'm leaving with nothing and I'm coming back to nothing. I mean, let's face it. I chased a guy. I chased a guy like I never thought I'd do because I thought he made me who I was. And maybe he did, but he's gone now, and who I am is no one, with nothing, not even a short list."

The Noah I know is going to say that I do have something, that I have everything I need: that I have my health and my family and my friends. But the Noah I know doesn't exist. The Noah I know probably never existed, because the real Noah, the Noah who is here now, says, "Why did you take me here?"

"To help me find Zan." It's the obvious, embarrassing answer.

"No, not here," he says, motioning vaguely in the distance. "I mean specifically *here*."

We've passed the row of apartments where I lived as a little kid, the white brick buildings with conifers standing tall and skinny, like tied-up Christmas trees. The building we're in front of now looks the same as it did back then, except it has a different name. "I don't think it's an ice factory anymore."

"This used to be an ice factory?" Noah stares at the bland stucco wall. "I never thought about that. About ice coming from factories. About where you'd even have an ice factory."

"When I was a kid, I mean a really little kid, my dad used to take me on walks here at night. Usually when I couldn't sleep. We'd take plastic cups from the shelf in the kitchen, and he would carry me on his shoulders. The outdoor drinking fountain had such cold water—pure, melted ice that sent shivers up and down my tongue. We would fill our cups to the top and drink and talk until it was so late it felt like morning." I sigh. "I don't know why I just told you that."

"Maybe we're finally getting to know each other," says Noah. "The way I've wanted to get to know you for a long time." He stops walking, so I stop walking, too. He puts his hand on my shoulder, and it's so different than when Zan put his hand on my shoulder. Zan's touch was heavy on my skin, making me tremble under the weight and passion of it. But Noah's hand feels like the last strokes of a paintbrush—just that gentle, just that fleeting.

When I look at him, all I feel is guilt. He's wanted to know me—tried to know me—and until I needed him, I shut him out completely. The same way I shut out everyone else outside of my circle of friends, outside of Zan.

"Zan's poem, that wasn't true about Haven being a cardboard world, was it?"

Noah's brows wrinkle, and his hand slides off my shoulder. "What do you mean?"

"I mean, we always felt like we were so different from the other kids in Haven. So much smarter, so much more sophisticated, so much . . . better. I just never put it into words the way Zan did tonight."

"Zan's an idiot."

"Yeah, I know. But I feel like maybe I . . . I was an idiot, too. I thought I was special, that I was the one person he thought was real. Everyone was cardboard but me. Then I find out he resented me as much as I resented everybody else in Haven. He was a jerk, but so was I."

"You weren't a jerk. You were just new in town. Looking for an identity. Finding friends. That's what every new kid at Haven goes through. I should know—I'm a Husky Ambassador." It's cheesy, but it makes us both smile.

"Want to go past my old elementary school?" The building isn't close enough to see yet, but it already smells like it did every day when I walked this path to school: shoe-scuffing blacktop and whiteboard markers and hot lunch. I know it's not possible, not really. But that doesn't stop the scent from spreading inside me, as strong as ever. "It's not far—just down that street."

"I'd like that," he says, and he sounds so happy about it, like of all the things we could possibly do, that would be his favorite. Zan never sounded like that about anything.

"Did Zan really ask you to keep me away from him?" I don't want to know the answer, but I have to.

Noah nods slowly. "He said you were obsessed. Which you were. But that was partly his fault. He left in all the wrong ways."

Zan didn't want me to find him. Part of me always knew that. But back then only the creases of my mind knew it. Now my whole body can feel it. With every pump from my ice-blood heart, I can feel how much he doesn't want me.

The school looks smaller than I remember it. The outside lights cast shadows over the peeling paint and the faded foursquare. "This is the new part," I tell him. "They built it when I was a fifth grader." We pass a net dangling from a basketball hoop by one lonely string. "The new part isn't very new anymore."

Noah shrugs. "It was new a long time ago."

The big plastic playset is so much shorter than it used to be. I pull myself to the top of the twisty slide, sitting on the eroded plastic planks at its base. Noah walks over to the Mini Zip Line.

"That's what everybody wanted to play on," I tell him.

It doesn't surprise me that Noah's chosen the most popular toy. I used to make fun of the kids who stood in line all recess waiting for a ride on it. They just wanted a turn because it was the cool thing to do, and I didn't do cool things, even then. I always thought it was because being a cool kid was beneath me. Now I think it's probably because the cool kids didn't like me. I mocked them out of self-defense.

What if, for the first time, a cool kid does like me? Not that he does. But what if?

Grabbing the bar, Noah pushes away from me, zipping into the night. He's heavy enough that he flies away.

Away, but not gone. He zips back to me.

Certain small thoughts click together in my mind. "Zan didn't buy me that poetry book, but his mom didn't either, did she?" I think about earlier, about Noah scribbling on his napkin.

Silence.

"You bought it, didn't you?"

He sighs. "We were playing basketball in my front yard. It was the only thing we ever really did together, you know? I knew your party was that night—Kristine invited me—and when I mentioned it to Zan he went off on his whole Haven-parties-suck spiel. I was all, 'Thanks a lot, man,' because it was a direct blow at me—he knew those were the kinds of parties I loved. Zan was always saying stuff like that, but every time I just convinced my-self he was kidding around."

"You're nicer than he is," I say, honestly.

"Nah. Just didn't want to fight. It wasn't that impor-tant. I mean, Zan and I'd been friends since we were little kids—shooting hoops kind of friends. But I always knew we'd never be real friends. He was never happy when he was with me, you know? Even back in the old days."

Was Zan happy when he was with me? Now it's so hard to remember.

"So it hurt me when he left, but it bugged me, too. I mean, he didn't even say good-bye. It was like, seriously, you can't even be bothered to say 'Hey, nice knowing you.' My good-bye is just a text saying 'keep Joy away from me.'"

Even when I've already heard them, the words ache like a sucker punch. But this isn't about Zan leaving me. This is about Zan leaving Noah.

"I shouldn't have been surprised he left how he did. Even that night, when he told me he was blowing off your birthday party and making up some bogus study group, it bugged me. I knew if you found out, it'd . . ." He does one pull-up on the bar hanging from the Zip Line, and then sends it sailing to the other end of the playground. "I just knew you couldn't find out. So I bought you the book."

"But . . . how did you know what to get me?"

Noah half grins. The happy part of grin is the half that's missing, though, so his expression is just a wilted upturn of his lips. "Did you honestly think no one else saw you? That everyone else was so clueless about who you were?" He stares at me, brows furrowed. He's really the one with thick, soulful Barry Manilow eyebrows. "It's like I said before. I knew you. I tried to, at least."

"Why?" I ask. In the darkness I can be honest. With him and with myself. "Why would you even want to know me? I was an utter and complete wench to you."

He laughs, and in the still air the sound travels forever. "Maybe I'm a glutton for punishment. Or maybe it's just because you weren't like the other girls."

And it's almost like we are any guy and any girl, walking in the night. Playing in the park. Flirting. And I know I'm fishing, but I can't help it, and I say, "Is that good or bad?"

"Good," Noah answers too automatically. Of course. Noah looks for—and finds—the good in everyone. Do I want more than that from him? I can't deny that I do.

"No," I say, shaking my head to prove it. "I mean different-from-the-other-girls special. Special like . . . not a service project."

"A service project?" Noah kicks up a flurry of wood chips from beneath him. "Like, the way I know the Husky Sub-4-Santa kids? Because I don't want to know any of them the way I know you. Not that they aren't awesome kids. They totally are."

"I believe you."

"Then I don't think I understand the question."

"I guess what I'm really asking is . . . that poem you read tonight, was it . . . true?" I'm embarrassed even as the words leave my mouth, but they keep coming. "I mean, I know the part about Zan was real, but was . . . all of it?"

Noah ducks his head and doesn't answer. Finally he says, "It's a song, actually."

"A song? Like, with music?" Most songs, of course, have music, but I'm too shocked to say anything else. My mind can't decide where to go. Since when does Noah write songs? Since when does Noah write songs about me? And which one am I supposed to be surprised about first?

I try to remember his exact lyrics, but it's hard to recall just what he said about me. I keep getting tripped up on the part where I find out Zan wanted to keep me away. What came after that? The rest of the song *felt* like Noah liked me, but now that I search for evidence of that in the actual words, I can't come up with any.

And, of course, Noah isn't saying anything.

I look up at him, try to find his eyes in the darkness. He feels me staring and looks back at me. For a too-long minute I look at him, and he looks at me, and it smells like school and old times and new times and we just keep staring until I figure it out.

Noah doesn't *like* me like me. He can't. Because maybe I'm not a service project. Maybe he did try to know me special, not service project special or everyone else special. Maybe he tried to know me special-special. And I proved to him that the only person I know how to be is Zan's girlfriend.

Now I'm not even that. Why would he want a girl who only knows how to be one thing? One thing she can't even hold onto—one thing she can no longer imagine holding onto? Who would want that kind of girl?

We are not any other guy and girl, walking in the night. Playing in the park. Flirting. We're just Joy and Noah. We will always be just Joy and Noah.

"We'd better get back," I whisper.

PEOPLE DON'T ASK ME
WHAT I MISS MOST

People don't ask me what I miss most about Haven, but what I miss most is what I never had.

In Haven, I never had Zan.

Not the way I wanted to.

I never had him. I miss him anyway.

WHEN GRETEL FINDS OUT

She just holds me. I can finally cry, so I do, and
she lets me.

THE HAPPIEST PLACE ON EARTH

Once, when Gretel and I were thirteen, our parents let us go to Disneyland by ourselves. In my foolish thirteen-year-old way I hoped we'd meet two guys: friends/brothers/cousins between the ages of thirteen and fifteen, funny and nice. Cute, too, but that was secondary. I wasn't picky. I was thirteen.

I spent the morning in a daze, imagining what it'd be like with a guy on Space Mountain, spinning through the darkness, holding hands hard, screaming with a smile that made my face hurt. When Gretel and I stopped for churros I imagined sharing one with him, each of us nibbling at one end until our lips met in the middle.

There were no guys that day, but by noon I'd forgotten about them anyway. It started raining and the park cleared out enough that Gretel and I rode Splash Mountain eight times in a row, until our clothes were heavy with rain and ride-water and we couldn't feel our toes.

We went into shops to warm up and tried on cone-shaped princess hats and safari fedoras. We didn't dry off that entire day, but it didn't matter.

Being soaked alone is cold. Being soaked with your best friend is an adventure.

ON THE ROAD AGAIN

It's too bright when we pack up the SAAB the next morning.

Gretel's there to send us off, even though it's Saturday morning and she could—should—be sleeping.

Noah adjusts his stupid Senior Discount cap. "Thanks for everything," he says, shaking Gretel's hand more firmly than he did when we got here.

"Have a safe trip," Gretel says. She stretches and yawns. "Call me, okay?"

"I will." The sun is still glinting, harsh, in all directions. My body is sore, every part of it: headache, tense neck, knotted shoulders. I feel a hundred years old.

Gretel's mom gives me a huge hug. "Thank you so much," I tell her.

"Anytime, sweetie. Tell your parents I send my love." She must feel me cringe, because she whispers: *"Don't worry, I won't say anything. Just be safe, okay?"*

"I will."

"I know." She keeps on hugging, even when I let go.

"Most of us have had an Alexander Kirchendorf in our lives," she says into my ear. "And we're all glad we didn't end up with him." She lets go, holds me at arm's length, and smiles.

I nod, and it hurts my back.

Noah holds the car door open for me. "Ready to go?"

I take one last look around. "Ready as I'll never be."

WISH LIST

It'd be easy to wish I'd never gone looking for Zan. And making a wish is easy—that's why it's a wish, not a reality. But that's not my wish.

And it'd be easy to wish that Zan had wanted me back. That it had been like I wanted it all along, that he saw me and knew, instantly, that we needed to be together. But that's not my wish.

I wish that last night we'd found Zan, and he'd smiled and waved us over. I wish that he'd been pleasant and congenial, and introduced us to his friends, none of whom he was "in a relationship" with. And maybe he would have been wearing flip-flops and maybe he wouldn't have, but it wouldn't matter either way, because in my wish I'd already decided.

I wish that Zan hadn't had to be a jerk for me to realize I didn't want him.

DO YOU KNOW WHO
MY FATHER IS?

It's been less than forty-eight hours since I traveled this same stretch of freeway. It feels like another lifetime. It feels like it was a different girl who sat in the front seat of this crazy old SAAB 900 and daydreamed about finding Zan and getting her life back, not realizing that it wasn't really a life at all. Not realizing that when they say "be careful what you wish for" it's not only true in cliché world. It applies to reality, too.

I can't think about this. I can't have an empty, blank mind today. Not today, when I don't have the luxury of exhausting my brain and falling asleep. I can't remember how to fall asleep.

"Do you want to play a game?" I ask Noah.

"What kind of game?" he asks, skeptical.

I shrug, "You know, one of those car games families play on long trips."

I see the beginnings of a smirk. "What, like the license-plate game?"

Every time I drive in California, I forget how quickly you can go from a major city to being thoroughly in the middle of nowhere. On this sunny Saturday morning just outside of Barstow in the Mojave Desert, we haven't passed another car for miles.

"Have you ever played My Father Owns a Grocery Store?"

He scrunches his nose. "Can't say that I have."

"Okay, so it goes like this. I start out, 'My father owns a grocery store, and in it he sells something that starts with the letter . . . C,'" I say, thinking of an item. "So then you try to guess what it is, asking yes or no questions."

"Is it a vegetable?" he asks, playing right along.

"Nope."

"A fruit?"

"Yep."

"Is it cantaloupe?"

Amazing. "You got it! In only two questions and one guess."

"Yeah," says Noah, sounding about fifteen times less impressed than I do. "Great game."

I wiggle a bit in my seat, trying to get comfortable. "Come on, you have to give it more than one round. It's your turn."

He sighs. Is it a sigh of irritation, or is he just breathing and I'm reading into it? Does it matter? No, it does not. It does not matter at all. So why am I thinking about it? Why do I notice?

"Um . . . my father owns a grocery store, and in it he sells something that starts with the letter *P*."

"Pumpernickel bread!" I blurt out.

"Uh, no." Noah's perplexed.

Not that I blame him. My reaction was, in a word, nutty. I explain. "Okay, so whenever my friends and I play this game, and it's Mattia's turn, she always, *always* chooses pumpernickel bread."

"Does she really like pumpernickel bread or something?" Noah sounds no less confused by my explanation.

"She's never even had pumpernickel bread! She just always chooses it." The longer I talk, the lamer it sounds. "Maybe you had to be there."

"Maybe so," Noah agrees, nodding; shaking it off.

But my own words stick with me:

Maybe you had to be there.

WHAT IF?

Our sleepovers were epic. The stuff of legends, really.

It's not like we ever decreed it: Mattia, Kristine, and I shalt have sleepovers every Friday night, and we shalt become known for it. It just started one weekend and became tradition.

The venue varied. We took turns hosting, except when Kristine's parents repainted the whole house and her place was out of commission for six weeks. We always made treats: peanut butter fudge, sugar cookies, frozen bananas dipped in chocolate.

Some nights we had movie marathons. Some nights we went on drive-bys. Some nights we even studied for tests together, making up flashcards and stupid mnemonic devices. But always, *always*, we played What If?

"You've never played What If?" asked Kristine, wide-eyed, at Charlotte's inaugural sleepover event. She said it like playing What If? was as common as wearing Chap-Stick, or visiting a shoe store.

Charlotte shook her head, eyes equally wide. "Nuh-uh. Is that bad?"

"No," I said, tearing sheets of paper into little squares. "It's easy to learn." We were at my house that night, sitting in a circle on my family-room rug. As hostess, I was in charge of preparing for the game.

Mattia gave everyone a pen. "First, you write down a question on the sheet of paper Joy gives you."

"A question starting with What if," said Kristine. "And it has to be a good one. Not like 'What if the Moors were never driven out of Spain?'"

She was talking about one disastrous weekend last spring, near the end of school, when a couple of random guys had raided a sleepover at Kristine's while we were playing What If? They insisted on joining in, and I called Zan begging him to come over, too.

The guys made a total mockery of the game, of course. I remember reading Zan's question and knowing it was his, recognizing his combination of caps and lowercase. At the time I rolled my eyes, throwing a crumpled piece of paper at his forehead. "Lame!"

But that night making fun of him was out of the question. It's easier to be loyal to someone who's far away. I said, "All guys are bad at What If?, not just Zan."

"Yeah, but Zan was the only one whose question was a *historical reference*," said Kristine, smirking.

Mattia was laughing, but Charlotte looked confused. She fiddled with her pen, drawing black lines across her palm.

"So, just stay away from school subjects," I continued, smiling at Charlotte so she'd relax and stop drawing before her hand became a giant black mass. "Then put your question in the middle of the circle. Then we all draw a question from the pile and answer it on a second piece of paper. The answers go in a separate pile. Then we each draw a random question and a random answer and read them out loud."

"It's funny, I promise," said Kristine, because Charlotte looked like she needed convincing.

"It really is," I seconded. "You'll see once we start playing."

Charlotte looked at me, nodded, and smiled. "I'm game," she said.

What if Mattia FINALLY stopped with the drive-bys?
Then I'd start singing "Mandy" at the top of my
lungs, baby!

What if Kristine actually hooked up with Rigby instead of
just threatening to?
In what universe would that even happen?

What if Joy got to meet Barry in person??

Then we would all simultaneously chant "Get thee hence, Satan!"

What if I hadn't been obsessed with Zan? What if I hadn't gone off to find him over UEA break? What if I was with my friends right now, frosting cookies and making fun of Mattia's taste in movies?

What if my mind hadn't left to find Zan months ago?

When you lose your best friend it's not always because they go somewhere, like Noah's best friend did. Sometimes you're the one who goes somewhere. What if you go somewhere and you don't know it?

How do you make it better when you went somewhere and you didn't know it then, but you do now?

LABEL MAKER

I was in the hospital once. For three days. I had to get my appendix out. I was eleven years old.

I had three different nurses. Two of them were the kind of nurses you think of when you think of nurses: gentle, smile-eyed ladies who look good in scrubs. One was a guy who looked just like Kramer on that show *Seinfeld*. He made jokes I didn't get and watched TV with me when he was bored. His name was Oliver.

The nurses had to track when I went to the bathroom, which is embarrassing at any age but mortifying when you're eleven. I was a good patient and told the nurses every time I went, just like I was supposed to. They never said anything about it, like it was the same as examining my IV or my heart rate.

Except Oliver. He told me, "You have an exceptionally large bladder, you know that?"

I did not know that. But at a time when it seemed like every other part of my body had something wrong with

235

it, I clung to the idea that one part of me not only worked, it was exceptional.

Thing is, I don't even know if I have an exceptionally large bladder anymore; after six years, maybe it's shrunk. Maybe Oliver didn't know what he was talking about in the first place. But it's still part of how I identify myself, part of what I think about when I think about who I am.

If I'd been standing on the stage at that dance recital, the voice above me would have said: Brunette. Confused. Exceptionally large-bladdered.

Zan's girlfriend. The voice would have said that, too, because being Zan's girlfriend was so much of me. And I worked for that label. I thought it made me better. It didn't, of course, didn't make me better or worse, but I still didn't want to let it go. I couldn't let it go. But now I can. Now I want to. Because it's not true.

THREE LITTLE WORDS

"If you could describe me in three words, what would they be?"

I ask Noah this completely out of the blue, so when his mouth opens immediately, I know it can't be good. Raising his nose in the air, he says, "Oh, I don't believe in labels." His high, affected voice sounds nothing like Ismene's, but the impression is still hilarious.

I have to wait to stop giggling before I say, "Seriously, though. Really think about it. If you only had three adjectives to tell the world who I am, which ones would you choose?"

I expect him to ask why I'm asking, but he doesn't. He's just quiet. The eleven o'clock sun is heating up the car with light like an Easy-Bake Oven, and at this point the sunglasses Noah wears are more like safety goggles. His hidden eyes make the quiet more unsettling than regular quiet, so I answer him even though he didn't ask.

"You know at the recital? How the narrator described each of the dancers?" I give him time to recollect, in case he's repressed the memory. "I was thinking about the words I'd use to describe myself then. How they're different than the words I'd use now."

I expect Noah to be proud of my emotional growth, to pat me on the shoulder or something, but he doesn't. He's just quiet. Finally he says, "I don't know. It's hard to describe someone in just three words. Impossible, maybe." He pauses. "Every word I think of sounds wrong."

I try to think of three words for Noah. "Nice" is too generic for him, even if it's accurate. As far as physical traits, "blue-eyed," of course. Maybe mention "vegetarian" for uniqueness?

But Noah's right. Because even though they're the three words I came up with, it's like I've just described a total stranger.

SOLID FOOD

I think the aching in my chest is hunger. Over the last fifteen hours I have forgotten how to distinguish different kinds of aching, but this one feels familiar enough that it might be hunger. I long to feel full.

As I see the green, white-lettered signs for Las Vegas on the side of the road, the number of miles getting smaller and smaller, I start formulating a plan. I need a plan. If I tell Noah I'm hungry, he'll just tell me to have snacks out of the duffel. If I tell him I want to stop in Vegas, he won't. So I bring it up all casual. "Noah, have you ever been to Las Vegas before?"

I still can't see his eyes behind the sunglasses and I still hate it. I hate not seeing how he's looking at me, or if he's looking at me, or how soft or hard his eyes are when he speaks. "Um . . . I think I think we might've stopped in Vegas on the way back from a family trip to Disneyland when I was little, but I don't remember. It might've been somewhere else. We needed food."

Even though Noah hasn't told me much about his

family, I can still imagine them in a silver minivan, the girls dressed up like Cinderella and Snow White, watching *Aladdin* on DVD. Saying "I'm hungry," and eating at a cheesy diner. The image isn't real, but it makes me smile anyway.

"What about you?" Noah asks back, because I guess I've been silent long enough that he realizes he should.

"Never been. Which is totally humiliating, because I used to live so close. Everyone goes to Vegas."

"Not everyone," he says, probably thinking about all the Mormons who think of Vegas as literal Sin City.

"But haven't you ever wanted to eat at a Vegas buffet?"

His eyebrows wrinkle, and I'm absolutely positive that behind those glasses, his eyes are rolling. "No, I've never wanted to eat at a Vegas buffet. I've never even thought about Vegas buffets."

"But buffets are the best part of Vegas for people who don't gamble!"

"Okay, what's with the Vegas buffet obsession?"

"I want to stop there for lunch. Please? We're way ahead of schedule."

"Can't we just go home? I'm exhausted. This trip hasn't exactly been relaxing . . . or—"

"Fun?" I interrupt. "This trip hasn't been relaxing or fun. And all trips are supposed to be one or the other:

relaxing or fun. I know from personal experience that seeing a bunch of half-naked dancers sounds like more fun than it is. Vegas buffets would be an upgrade."

Noah laughs. Making him laugh makes me feel better.

"I mean, what are we going to say when people ask us what we did over the break? Tell them we drove to California, stayed there one day, got burned by our former friend, and then went home? Are we seriously that pathetic?"

I can see Noah creating a scene in his head. He gets the same look I get. "'So, Noah, what you do over UEA?' 'Went to Vegas, baby!'"

"Yes! That's *exactly* what I'm talking about. Living it up." Living at all. Because I feel like I'm not living at all. I feel like ice has been running through me since last night at the poetry reading and that if I'm not careful, I'll freeze solid.

But I can't freeze solid, not now, not deep in desert with warm streaming in on me from all sides and the bicep of my right arm turning pink. I will not allow myself to freeze solid in the sun.

"So are we going to live it up? Because to be honest, I need to eat. I haven't had anything since . . ." I trail off, because I can't remember the last time I ate something. "Lunch yesterday. At the Ballad."

"You haven't eaten since lunch yesterday?"

"Unless you count the hot chocolate from open-mike night."

"I don't." Noah pauses. "Do you think they have vegetarian options?"

"Of course," I say like it's obvious, even though really, how would I know? "And they'll definitely have Sprite. Including all the free refills you want. In fact, it will all be free. I'll pay." I owe him a heck of a lot more than a meal at a Vegas buffet, but it's the best I can do.

"We'll go Dutch," says Noah.

GOING TO VEGAS, BABY!

From the freeway, the Strip looks like it does on postcards and in movies. Here you are, driving through miles and miles of nothing, and then there's this carnival in front of you, appearing like a mirage.

The landscape is familiar, even though it's one I'm seeing for the first time. And for some reason, that comforts me. It's a place I know but also don't know and that's just about right. "Let's park in one of those big Strip hotel parking lots. Then we can look around for somewhere to eat."

Noah nods. "This exit?"

"Sure."

The streets in Las Vegas are as crowded now as they are in every movie about Vegas. "Where do I go?" asks Noah.

"The first place you can go, go there."

We end up in a hotel parking lot surrounded by an insane amount of palm trees.

"Do palm trees even grow in Vegas?" Noah asks, pulling into the garage. "Or are they yet another part of Vegas that's fake?"

"Of course they're real. Do you think they would bother putting up this many plastic palm trees?" I can't keep that certain tone I use with Noah out of my voice. I've grown kind of fond of that "duh" tone.

Noah starts laughing. "I didn't mean they were plastic," he says, finally. "I meant do they grow here as native plants, or did Vegas have to introduce them to the environment?"

"Oh." By the time I realize I'm embarrassed, I'm already blushing. "Right."

Noah smiles, but doesn't say anything. "Should we check out the buffet in this hotel?"

The buffet is, of course, located in the middle of the casino, and I am petrified that someone is going to spot us, notice how young we are, and cart us off to wherever it is they take underage gamblers.

"Why do you keep looking up?" asks Noah, after I stumble into him for the third time.

"Checking for surveillance cameras. There are cameras everywhere in Vegas."

"*Hidden* cameras," Noah says. "Don't you think security might find it suspicious that you're actually searching them out?"

"Fine." I look back down and I see we've gotten to the buffet. On the other side of the thick glass facing us, fancy dessert trays and a cotton-candy machine shine.

"You ready for this?" asks Noah, seeing the way the food beckons me.

I stretch my arms in front of me, then behind me. "Oh, I was born ready."

MY MEAL AT THE BUFFET

Round 1

Pineapple/ham pizza

Tomato/green pepper pizza

Garlic knot

Pulled pork

Mac 'n' cheese

Sweet potatoes

Round 2

Bow-tie pasta with aribiatta
    (half marinara, half red pepper) sauce

Fried rice

Baked root vegetables

Shrimp lo mein

Round 3

Stuffing

Cornbread pudding

Collard greens

Mashed potatoes

Corn on the cob

Pork ribs with barbecue sauce

Dessert

Mini pineapple upside-down cake

Tart with fresh berries

Chocolate chip muffin

Cinnamon-sugar doughnut

ALL THAT REMAINS

I eat. I eat and I eat and I eat and do not stop. I do not stop to talk to Noah. I do not stop to take proper breaths. If I stop I might realize I'm no longer hungry, and if I realize I'm no longer hungry, I'll have to admit to myself that all the buffets in Las Vegas won't fill the hole in my heart.

"You miss Zan, don't you?" Noah asks quietly.

Zan. Just the split-second sound of his name rubs up against my freshly scraped insides.

I look at Noah, look at the crescent-moon of crust left on his plate. It reminds me of Homecoming, of pizza back when he was just Noah Talbot, some guy I didn't know or want to know. Back then he would have said, "You miss Zan, don't you?" and I would have said, "Of course I miss Zan, you idiot."

But that time is long past now. Now Noah says, "You miss Zan, don't you?" and I say, "Kinda," because I do miss Zan, but he's mean. He's so, so mean I shouldn't miss him. He's so, so mean I'm wondering if I remember him right, or if I made it all up. Because how can things go from right to wrong so quickly?

"How can something start out so good and turn out so bad?" I don't mean to say it out loud, but I don't mind that I've said it out loud. The tables here are high, and the chairs, too, so my feet dangle midair.

Noah shrugs. "How can something start out so bad and turn out so good?"

I swing my feet. "What do you mean?"

"Well." Noah smoothes out his napkin, its creamy white stained an orange-red. "Like with us. We started out maybe not so good. But I think of us now and I think . . . we're good."

"I guess it works that way, too. I guess the whole world is made up of things coming together and things falling apart."

"But this thing with Zan, this thing falling apart, it's more important than anything getting put together?"

"What?" Is he talking about him and me? Is he talking about us coming together? As friends? As more? I search his face for clues, but I can't read him.

Then I hear something, and I tell my thoughts to be quiet, and I listen harder and I hear it. The woman on the radio is singing "Loving you is easy 'cause you're beautiful." I think about Alex/Zan, back when he was just Zan and still beautiful to me, how he still is and will always be beautiful, easy to love. There are parts of him that are ugly—big, ragged chunks of him that are ugly. But that little leftover beautiful part—that's enough to make him easy to love.

I'll always love him, and I always thought that made me so much better than the other girls with their weak love. Maybe it doesn't, though. Maybe it'd be better if I could stop loving him. If I don't, will I ever be able to love somebody else?

"Do you hear that?" I say, but Noah just shakes his head and by then the song's drifted into a bunch of "la-la-la-la-na-nah's" anyway so that doesn't help. "Never mind. I guess we better get back on the road."

"Yeah," says Noah, crumpling his napkin back up. "Let's go."

AN ANSWER TO PRAYER

I never think about things like cars starting.

I mean, it's obvious that I'm not a car person from the fact I didn't give Noah's classic car a second thought. Maybe Mattia's Rabbit is also a classic, and instead of being annoyed by its shortcomings, I should be impressed that a classic like that still runs. But I'm not. I don't think about cars running.

Until they don't.

Which is the case when Noah starts the car after we have lunch. He puts the key in the ignition, turns it, and nothing happens. I don't notice, because I'm all into my navigator routine, in which I buckle up, consult the atlas, and otherwise look official and pay zero attention.

"What's wrong with the SAAB?" asks Noah, as if I will miraculously know.

To remind him that I'm not a car person, I say, "Something's wrong with the SAAB?"

Noah's eyebrows crinkle. "Yeah, something's wrong.

The car's not starting." He tries the key again. There's not even a choking-false-start start-up sound. Nothing.

I try to be helpful. "Maybe you should check under the hood."

"Maybe. It's just usually not engine problems if the car won't even start." He scratches his head, like you see in old-timey sitcoms, and I can't help laughing.

"This isn't funny, Joy!" he says loudly, and I look over at him. His eyes have frozen over. In fact, I've never seen them so frosty—like two Minnesota lakes in January. We've seen each other at our bed-headed best. We've driven for hours on end, just us. We've been yelled at by Ultimate-Frisbee pseudojocks. We've been trashed in a bad poem. We've taken moonlight walks and consumed mass quantities of food together. I've never see him look like this.

So I think of it from his perspective. I am interested in cars. I am interested in the SAAB 900 in particular. I am interested in *my* SAAB 900 in most particular. My SAAB 900 is having mechanical difficulties. *And* I'm in Vegas. All I can think about is how to fix my baby.

After I've channeled my inner Noah, I say "I'll check the owner's manual," and flip open the glove box while he checks under the hood.

The owner's manual turns out to be more confusing than my AP biology textbook. I have to keep leaning out the car door and asking things like: "What's the chassis? How many cylinders does the car have, and does it matter?" Also, the owner's manual is falling apart, so I can't open it all the way without the spine giving out.

"Put back the manual," Noah demands, after I inform him about the car's apparent lack of safety features. His tone softens. "Just say a prayer for us, okay?"

It's a very Noah Talbot, Soccer-Lovin'-All-Around-Good-Mormon-Boy thing to do. But it's also a very Joy Afterclein thing to do. Some things can be both, and prayer is one of them. Prayer fits everybody. This I believe.

So I pray. I pray that the SAAB can start, that we can get home from this trip safely, that I can stop loving Zan so much that I can't love anything else. That I can figure out who I am without him, what I want to be without him. That I can stop thinking about him every second of every minute of every hour. That he can stop invading my thoughts even when I'm thinking about something— someone—else. Then I remember I'm supposed to be praying about our ride home, so I ask again for the SAAB to start. Amen.

BAD NEWS BEARS

God answers prayers in His own way and in His own time. It's the first thing they teach you in Primary. His answer to this prayer?

You guys are on your own on this one. At least for now.

Noah slinks into the front seat, dejected. "I have no idea what's wrong. Or how to fix it." He bangs his head against the steering wheel, but I know better than to laugh. "We're going to have to get it towed. Not to mention repaired."

I stare at the back of his blond head, seeing all the strands up close, wondering what it'd be like to touch them. I sigh. "Bad news bears."

He lifts his head and stares at me. "What did you say?"

"Bad news bears." It occurs to me that I'm not sure where I picked up this phrase, or where it comes from. "It means something not good has happened."

"I know what it means!" Noah is mad now. This is the closest I've ever heard him to yelling. "I mean, not because I've ever heard it before, but because I figured it out. Why would you say that?"

"I don't know, I think I heard someone say it as a kid, although I don't know where they got it from—"

"That's not what I mean!" The tirade continues. "I mean, why would you say that *now*? This is a crisis, not bad news bears! My car was in perfect condition, and I don't know what happened."

It's actually frightening to see him this upset. Noah Talbot, so relaxed, so easygoing, so . . . opposite of me. Here he is flying off the handle and getting obsessed so . . . like me. Freaky.

I know what this means. This means I have to step up to the plate, take one for the team, all those sports metaphors that mean I need to take care of this for him like he's taken care of so many things for me.

"Listen, I'm sorry." I put my hand on his shoulder. Only because that's what taking one for the team means, of course. Not for any other reason.

He shrugs it away. I don't know whether it's because he's upset still, or because he doesn't want me touching him.

I decide it doesn't hurt my feelings. I decide the short, stabby pain inside me isn't really there. "I know I should have taken this more seriously. I know the SAAB's your baby. So look at it this way—we're on the Strip, not in the middle of nowhere. I'll call a mechanic, get a tow service, and this will all get taken care of . . ." I search for the right phrase. "Lickety-split. This will all get taken care of lickety-split."

It works, and he smiles.

"Now, do you want to come inside with me, where it's cool, while I get some numbers and make some calls?"

"Can I just stay out here?" Noah strokes the dashboard, in a gesture loving enough to make my expression soften. Even for a car.

"I'll be right back."

FOREIGN TERRITORY

I've said it before and I'll say it again: I'm not a car person. But when I think of foreign cars, I think of these: Lamborghini. Mercedes-Benz. BMW. I do not think of the SAAB 900.

Thing is, it turns out that all those people who are car people do consider the SAAB a foreign car. And that would be totally fine with me. I'd say, hey, you go on thinking what you think, I'll go on thinking what I think, and we'll be just fine. Except that all these people who think SAABs are foreign cars refuse to fix them.

Also, auto mechanics are some of the most unhelpful people on the planet. After summers spent as a part-time receptionist for my dad, I know how to do phone calls—but evidently these guys don't. It takes me seven—yes, *seven*—calls to track down a mechanic who a) works on foreign cars, b) works on SAABs, and c) is open weekends. The soonest he can get the car back to me? Tomorrow. As in, one night and one day from now.

Fortunately, I have a plan. Unfortunately, I think it's going to go over worse than my buffet idea did.

Especially when I hear Noah's reaction to the news we're not leaving here anytime soon.

"Tomorrow?" He sputters. "What are we supposed to do tonight? It's not even three in the afternoon yet, and they're so sure they can't fix it today?"

"They close at five," I say, unhelpfully.

"I don't have a credit card," says Noah. "I'm going to have to use all the cash I have to fix the SAAB. We have nowhere to stay. We're homeless!"

I feel my cue to step in. "We're not homeless, Noah. Get a grip."

"Why? Do *you* have a credit card?"

"Yes, but it's only for emergencies." I bite my lip.

"This *is* an emergency!"

"Yes, but . . . well, my parents pay it off for me. That's why it's only for emergencies. I don't want them to get a huge bill while I'm living it up in Las Vegas."

"Living it up? You're just getting a place to sleep!" A look of realization crosses his face. "This isn't about the money, is it? You just don't want your mom and dad to know we stopped in Las Vegas."

"So? Would you want your parents to know?"

"My parents don't even know I went to California," he

admits. "They think I went to Brad Sidle's condo in Park City."

"What?"

"I know, I know. I should have told them the truth. I just couldn't. It seemed . . . I don't know, too weird."

I wonder which part he thinks is weird: going to California, or going to California with me. No matter what, he didn't tell his parents, though. We're partners in crime. Who'd have thought? "I told my parents I was with Charlotte."

He nods, and of course there's no lecture like I would have expected if he hadn't been the first to admit he lied, too. "So where does all this leave us?"

"Well, I have a plan, which you may or may not like."

"Shoot," he says.

"Since we're technically too young to rent a room in this city anyway, I think the only place we could check into is somewhere without a casino. When I was looking up mechanics, I got a brochure at the front desk for Lucky Seven Motel. The rooms are cheap enough that I could pay for one with the money I have left. Then we wouldn't have to charge it."

"Pay for *one*? For us to share?"

"Right. We'd get two beds." I give him a small smile.

"Except that it'd be a motel! With a girl! Do you know

how much trouble I'd be in if anyone knew I took a girl to a *motel*?"

"You're not taking me. I'm paying, so I'm taking you."

"Like that's better!"

"I'm open to other options," I tell him, because I know there aren't any.

"You take the room. I'll sleep outside."

"Maybe you can get one of those inflatable lounge chairs and spend the night floating in the pool."

"I'm serious."

"That's why it's so ridiculous. Let's be reasonable here. We can only afford one room. We're not romantically involved. We're just doing what we have to do. This is a unique situation."

"We couldn't have predicted it. It's almost unavoidable."

"Almost? It's completely unavoidable."

"Okay, fine. Let's try it."

"Okay. Fine."

The sign on the wall of the Lucky Seven front office says: ABSOLUTELY NO LOCALS. The desk attendant's name is Ruth, and she has an accent. It sounds like a cross between German and Spanish. "You'd like a room, yes?"

Before I can answer, Noah asks her why locals can't check in.

"The locals who stay here? Either hookers or dealers. Trash the rooms. Never leave."

"Oh." I know that he wishes he hadn't asked.

"We'd like a room for tonight, please. Nonsmoking with two queens." I hope I sound polite and mature, in case they have a rule against teenagers, too.

"Rooms come in two types: two beds, double, or one bed, queen. No two queens."

I've never stayed anywhere this cheap, and maybe I am just as sheltered as the Havenites in their cardboard world, but I'm starting to think that's not necessarily a bad thing. "Okay, then nonsmoking, two beds."

Ruth checks the computer, an outdated PC with a fat monitor. "Only nonsmoking room left has one bed."

I look at Noah. "A smoking room, then," I say, and he nods in agreement.

The look on Ruth's face tells us that won't work, either. "Only empty room with two beds has bad electricity," she says.

Noah and I share an alarmed look. Bad electricity? I don't even want to *know* what that means. "Um, we don't want the room with bad electricity," I say, looking at Noah, who nods. "Sounds dangerous."

"Then best bet is 14A. Nonsmoking, one bed."

I sigh. Maybe this is God's way of testing my commitment to abstinence. A test I will pass with flying colors.

"Fine." I'm tired and bewildered and want to get off my feet. "We'll take 14A."

"Thank you for your business," she says. "Take some brochures."

I look over to the rack against the wall, where Noah is already looking at a pamphlet for a water park. "This looks cool," he says.

"Noah, come on." I grab his sleeve. "We have to go." I turn to Ruth. "Thank you for your help."

"Enjoy your stay," says Ruth, going back to her romance novel.

HOME SWEET HOME

"I'm horrible with card keys," I say, trying to make the little green light approve our entrance into 14A.

"Here." Noah flips the card around and guides my hand. We slide the card in and out in a split second, and we get the go-ahead. "After you," he says, holding open the door with his free hand.

"Thanks." I set down my duffel and look around. "This actually seems pretty nice."

"Yeah, not bad. It's got logo pens *and* Lucky Seven sticky notes." He makes sure I'm looking at him. "Catch!" he says, tossing me one.

"Thanks." I shoot him a thumbs-up and drop the notepad in my purse, still looking around. "Complimentary plastic cups and an ice bucket. Definite high class."

"Oh, definitely. Free local calls, cable, and"—he opens the top drawer—"the Bible."

"Can't go wrong with that," I say, although I'm pretty

sure Noah has his Bible/Book of Mormon combination tucked into his backpack.

"I got a free map while I was checking out the brochures," Noah says. "Did you know that we're technically still on the Strip, although the tow-truck company took us about three hundred miles from where the car was parked?"

I fumble for the remote and flip on the TV. It's playing an original movie on Lifetime. Sweet. I could use a little madwoman estrogen about now. "Yeah, the brochure for this place boasted about its 'prime Strip location.'" I make the air quotes, of course. How could I not?

"Well, I think that, since we're here, we should . . . you know, peruse our environs."

I turn off the TV to make sure I heard him. Lifetime movies are all alike, anyway. "Peruse our environs? You're not talking about that water park, are you? Because that's a big thumbs-down."

"I'm talking about checking out the Strip. The *real* Strip. The sights."

"You want to see the sights?" Noah, who had to be coaxed into even stopping here for lunch, now wants to go gallivanting around?

"Why are you acting like it's so crazy that I want to see the sights? We're here; we should get out and do something. Live it up." He makes this half-groaning sound. "Plus, I need to walk off the buffet."

God has answered my prayers, in His often baffling but infinitely inspired way. To heal my broken heart, he has sent me the ultimate in American distractions: a night in Las Vegas. "Just let me get my shoes."

MY FAVORITE
LAS VEGAS SIGHTS

The last few minutes we catch of the skanky/ cheesy pirate vs. siren show at TI, because I love to see how nervous it makes Noah.

The dancing fountains erupting to "Hey, Big Spender" in front of the Bellagio.

The mini-Eiffel Tower glowing in twilight as we pass Paris.

The prominent, slightly gaudy but oddly patriotic Statue of Liberty at New York-New York.

NOAH'S FAVORITE
LAS VEGAS SIGHTS

The free tram between TI and the Mirage.

The eels in the aquarium behind the front desk at the Mirage. (He says they're amazing; I say they're just eels.)

The animatronic statues inside Caesars Palace. The statues look like real marble, until they start moving and retelling old sea lore. ("They're probably coated in latex," Noah muses. Who but Noah muses about attractions in an overpriced hotel mall?)

Posing next to someone dressed up like the green M&M and getting our picture taken at—where else?—M&M's World (photo courtesy of Noah's camera phone).

The thing is, you see the Strip on a map—say, the free map you picked up at the Lucky Seven Motel—and it doesn't look that long. You get in front of the big hotels and it still doesn't seem that far. It's like, "oh, the Bellagio is right next door to Caesars Palace, no big deal."

Only it is a big deal. Because eventually, even though you haven't gone all the way down the Strip yet, your feet start to give out. Also, you begin to feel dirty. Physically dirty. It's like the cigarette smoke and taxi exhaust and tar from the construction on every corner have become part of you.

Noah and I have reached this point by the time we get to M&M's World. Besides, it's been hours. I think. I can't remember what time we left, and I'm not sure what time it is now, but it was light then and now it's dark.

"Can we take a cab back?" I ask Noah.

"Yes, please," he says.

BAILING OUT

When we get back, the room is coated with shadows. "Dibs on the shower!" says Noah, running to the bathroom and slamming the door.

I start rummaging through my backpack for bedtime supplies when I hear the shower turn on. My Barry shirt is beyond wrinkled and my pajama pants have a chocolate ice-cream stain running down the leg. I've just found my hairbrush when I hear the shower turn off. I'm watching some Chinese game show when Noah says: "Joy, were you planning on taking a shower this evening?"

I can hardly hear him through the door, so I mute the TV. "A shower? No. I'm hoping to let the Las Vegas stench seep deep into my skin so I can smell like a showgirl forever." I hop off the bed and over to the bathroom door.

"Listen, this is no time to be cute. If you intend to take a shower tonight, we've got to think of something."

"What? Um . . . can I come in?"

He opens the door, and without meaning to, I inhale, fast. He looks fantastic: he's standing there, wearing the official T-shirt of the Haven High Boys' Soccer Team, and the humidity makes it cling to his chest. His hair is still wet and the strands seem to separate by color: light, lighter, lightest. He smells like strong soap and shaving cream. His skin looks so soft that it makes me ache that I can't touch it. "So what's wrong?"

"This." He points to the bathtub. "It won't drain." The tub is still three-quarters of the way full.

"The drain is clogged," I tell him. "Should I try to fix it?" I'm not so great with the hands-on-fixing stuff, which he knows.

"What, you think I'm inept? I already tried to fix it myself."

"I know, I know, but I have to at least give it a shot. My hygiene depends on it." I'm thinking that in a motel as seedy as this one, there might be hair in the drain, which is totally disgusting but something I know how to fix. I take a deep breath and swallow hard to get my hormones under control.

The shower curtain is this tacky industrial-strength beige, and I push it aside, swirling my hands in the soapy water, trying not to think that it is the very water that has touched him. All of a sudden, I miss him, strong. It doesn't make sense, of course; he's right here, what's to miss? Besides, all I'm doing is staring into dirty water, not reliving some great memory. So why am I overcome with the emotion I only know as missing someone?

There's no clog, as far as I can tell. The drain's wide open—by all logic, water should be making a hasty retreat. "Maybe we can call maintenance."

"It's almost midnight. I doubt maintenance is on call."

Oh. Right. "I forgot about the time." I can only think of one other option. "I guess we'll have to drain it ourselves. I'll grab the ice bucket."

"The ice bucket! Stroke of genius!" He smacks his hand to his head. "Why didn't I think of that?" His eyes shine with respect and something else, some deeper look I can't place. His face has this chiseled look, like the strong curve of his jawline is sculpted from granite. Coupled with his tight abs and blond hair, he looks like a philosophy-major-turned-male-model.

"You should go get the ice bucket now," he says.

"Oh. Yes. Sorry."

"Let's get an assembly line going," says Noah. "I'll fill the bucket and hand it to you, you dump it down the sink. Does that work?"

"Yep."

Noah fills up quickly and when he gives me the bucket I stagger under its weight.

This amuses him. "You got that?"

"What, you think I'm weak?"

"No, not weak, just . . ."

"Don't finish that sentence," I say, tossing the bucket at him.

Of course he catches it, no problem. "Not weak. Anything but weak." After about two minutes he tells me the tub is almost empty.

"It's all yours." He holds the bathroom door open for me and smiles.

I take a cold shower.

One problem: I was in such a hurry to get in the shower, that I neglected something. Barry shirt? Check. Chocolate-stained pajama pants? Check. Clean underwear? Check. Bra? Um, no.

Usually this wouldn't be a big deal—I'm used to sleeping without my bra on. But when I'm sharing a room with a boy, particularly Noah Talbot? I'm not so much used to that. It would be worse to go out of the bathroom in only a towel to retrieve said bra, however. I dry off and dress as quickly as I can.

The TV's still set to the Chinese game show station when I get back into the room. Noah does not look happy. He stares at my chest, and I cross my arms instinctively. Are my nipples poking out?

"Nice," he says.

I blush. No way he's referring to what I think he's referring to, because Noah Talbot talking dirty would shake my faith in all guys, everywhere, and besides—my 34A chest isn't all that nice.

"You weren't kidding," he says, apparently oblivious. "You really are a Fanilow."

I glance at my shirt, sigh at my foolishness, and smile. "Would I joke about a thing like that?" My hair is still wet so I twist it into a bun and secure it with one of those cloth ponytail-holders that don't yank your hair. I'm definitely not up for blow-drying tonight. "Why'd you look so upset before? Chinese game show got you down?"

"Nope, nothing to do with the excellent viewing options here," says Noah. "But other amenities are lacking. There aren't any extra blankets in the closet."

"So what?"

"So what am I going to do if I get cold?" Looking over, I see that he's already laid a pillow on the floor next to the desk.

"Noah," I say, turning my body away from him so he can only see my back, "don't sleep on the floor. The bed's big enough for both of us." I know it doesn't sound right, but I can't think of another way to put it. I wish we had two beds, or at the very least, a king, but it is what it is.

"Are you sure?"

"Yes. Nothing will happen. We both know that." I fold

down the blankets on my side of the bed and hop in. The bedspread's not too bad—a striped satin-wannabe that's probably polyester. But the blanket underneath feels like felt.

Nothing will happen. I have to admit it makes me wonder what it'd be like if something did happen. Not that I'm a nympho or anything. I'm one hundred percent willing to wait. It's just . . . I've never had the possibility as real as it is right now.

I mean, it isn't real—not really. Noah would never let it happen, even if he wanted to. And I have no idea how close or far away he is from wanting to. He hasn't so much as accidentally brushed against me since last night. He didn't even let me pat him on the shoulder all buddy-buddy. "Trust me. We'll survive this night with virtue intact. Even if we share a bed."

Noah picks up his pillow.

"Really, I'm sick of this being an issue," I say, trying not to watch him too carefully as he slides into the other side of the bed. "Because it's a nonissue, right?"

"Right." It sounds like he's so close to me, when I know for a fact we aren't touching.

This is what temptation feels like, having him lying here next to me, in his tight shirt and warm-ups, looking vulnerable and yes, sexy as heck.

He turns off the lamp over his head, and the room goes darker than dark. The blackout curtain on the window means business.

I can't breathe. "It's really no big deal, anyway," I say, hoping the words will steady my heart rate.

"Yeah. No big deal."

Not only can I hear him talk, I can feel him talk. I want to turn around and touch his face. I want him to touch my hair. I want to hear that he wants us to be more than friends, that he wants me. That he's glad we went on this trip and glad Zan and I are over.

But he doesn't. Neither one of us says anything.

Later that night, when I wake up to go to the bathroom, Noah is curled on the floor next to the desk.

DREAM SEQUENCE

I am dreaming. It is that point in dream when you know it's a dream. You know it's temporary. You still don't wake yourself.

This isn't like my other dreams, though. There's no story line, no setting, no characters. There's only Noah. There's only Noah, and he looks so good and so soft and so right. I'm not in the dream, but my body can feel him, and he feels so good and so soft and so right.

It's the kind of dream that makes me feel like I have a thousand times more blood than I usually do, and my veins are much closer to my skin than they usually are, and the gallons of blood are racing through my surface-level veins faster than I can even breathe.

It's the kind of dream that makes me glad I don't believe that dreams predict the future anymore. The future this dream predicts is highly inappropriate for a girl who won't even watch R-rated movies.

It's the kind of dream I never had about Zan.

THE MORNING AFTER

"Hey, Sleepyhead," Noah says as I stretch awake.

Has he been watching me sleep? The thought makes me excited, but is too weird to contemplate further. Besides, if he *has* been watching me sleep, he's been doing other things, too. He's already fully dressed, with his stuff packed up and his extra pillow put away. He's swirling his key chain around his finger while he smiles at me.

"What time is it?" I ask. I'm afraid he'll see my body reacting to him. I look away for good measure, glancing at the readout on the digital clock.

"Eleven fifteen?" I bolt out of bed, forgetting that I'm braless. "Why'd you let me sleep so late? We're supposed to be out of here by now. I've got to get dressed and finish packing and call a cab." I step to the right, then the left, unsure of what to do first.

"Calm down." Noah takes me by both wrists—definitely not helping me to calm down any. It's a new day, and Noah is touching me again. His hands are warm, and just the right not-quite-rough-not-quite-smoothness.

"Don't worry." He's still smiling. "Checkout isn't until noon, so you have plenty of time to change and pack up. I thought you deserved to sleep in. And we don't need to call a cab, remember?" He holds up his key chain as proof. "It's already taken care of. Needed a new fuel pump." By the way he keeps grinning, I'm guessing a fuel pump is one of the less expensive things that can go wrong with a SAAB 900.

"So, we're . . . good?" I ask.

"We're good. Go get ready. I'll watch *SportsCenter* while you're gone." Noah smiles again, releasing my wrists. "Okay?"

I nod. "Hey, Noah, thanks for . . ." I'm not quite sure how to finish. *Thanks for taking care of all this* is too strangely intimate. *Thanks for everything* is too generic and greeting-card-esque. Nothing is right. "Thanks for waiting until I'm out of the room to watch *SportsCenter*."

TRIBUTE

"I have a surprise for you," says Noah, after we've gotten in the SAAB and resumed our driver/navigator roles.

"You do?" I fiddle with my seat belt. It's already so unbelievably bright that I lower my sun visor.

"Yeah. I felt really bad about yesterday. About freaking out on you about the car and stuff. I wanted to make it up to you."

"Seriously? You've made it up to me like a hundred times already just by going with me on this trip."

He smiles.

"Besides, you're talking to a girl who once freaked out after she accidentally put her paperbacks on the same shelf as her hardcover books. I'm used to freak-outs. I mean, think about it. My whole life is a freak-out."

"Maybe I'm trying to change that," says Noah.

"Maybe you are changing that," I say, and I think my words come out a little flirty, even though I don't want them to. Or at least, I wish I didn't want them to. "When do I get to find out what the surprise is?"

He sails past the corner where we're supposed to turn right and get back onto the freeway. "Right now. You see, we're not going home. At least, not yet."

"Okay." It's more like two words: Oh. Kay. Where could Noah be taking me? Only one thing comes to mind. "Wait, are we going to church?" Mormon chapels are all over the place, and it usually isn't too hard to find one. But we're both seriously underdressed. "I don't have any church clothes with me."

"We're not going to church," says Noah. I expect him to be sad about it, but I'm detecting the beginnings of a smile. "I don't have church clothes, either. Don't worry, the Lord knows our hearts. Today we'll worship Him in our own way."

A week ago I would have been shocked if Noah Talbot said something like that. Noah Talbot, letter-of-the-law obedient. I know better now. No one's that easy to figure out. No one's a cardboard cutout. No one will always act the way you expect them to.

"We are going to see firsthand the talent with which God has blessed His children." Noah taps his fingers on the steering wheel in some unknown rhythm. "We are going," he says, his grin getting wider with each word, "to see Barry Manilow."

The first thing I think is: You didn't have money for two hotel rooms, but you have money for two Barry Manilow concert tickets? Then I think how the show must have sold out weeks ago. Then I think about how it's the middle of the day. "What do you mean? See him like see where he performs or something? Because really, as surprises go, that's a little on the lame side."

"Good thing that's not it, then." Even in the sunlight, Noah's not wearing sunglasses. His eyes are beautiful in this light. In this light, they literally twinkle.

"So are you going to tell me or what?"

He brakes for a red light, opens the glove box, and hands me a brochure. "I picked it up at the front desk yesterday."

I look it over. On the front is, indeed, a picture of Barry Manilow. Upon closer inspection, however, I realize that it isn't Barry Manilow. Bold yellow lettering reads: RATED BEST TRIBUTE SHOW IN VEGAS!

The Barry concert is in a fairly big name Strip hotel, so I have high hopes that it will be a decent show. I figure the theater will be big enough to stand out, too. But that's where I'm wrong. Looking at the "You Are Here" map in the casino, I see that the place is designed like a castle from the Middle Ages—the moat that runs the perimeter is actually a mall, and the fortress, where the "entertainment venues" are, is deep inside. We pass every bath-and-body store known to man, lingerie stores I haven't even heard of, and windows advertising sale prices higher than I'd spend on splurges.

It takes about a dozen turns and fifty or so switchbacks to get where we need to be. The entertainment area is a cavern designed to look like the outside, so we can see a pale blue sky and puffy white clouds while we stand in line for general admission. Apparently the Barry show is shoved in between "Esmeralda, the Kid-Friendly Hypnotist" and some presentation of amazing pet tricks.

"This is kind of a dive," says Noah. "I was thinking it'd be . . . cooler."

"You thought a Barry Manilow tribute show would be cool? What's wrong with you?"

We're in Vegas, and we're standing in a line that looks like the check-in counter at the airport. It isn't a cool, Vegas-style line—there's no bouncer, no velvet rope, no security guy to joke around with. We're in Vegas, and we're standing between two gigantic ladies with fanny packs and a geriatric couple with matching walkers.

This is how Noah and Joy do Las Vegas.

The thing is, I don't mind. Not even a little.

The theater itself isn't any better. It's not even a theater, really—my middle school auditorium had a nicer setup. A bunch of padded folding chairs are set up in bleacherlike rows.

"Seriously?" Noah looks around in dismay. "Good thing I got these tickets half off." He sits down gingerly and whispers to me, "I feel bad for the poor suckers who paid full price. I can't believe they have the nerve to charge forty-six bucks a ticket for this."

"Forty-six dollars? How do they sleep at night?" The lights are already starting to dim—I guess Barry needs to get over and done with quick-like, before the performing beagles do their thing. "This better be a dang good show."

I can't get over the math, though. Half price on forty-six dollars means he spent twenty-three dollars on me. Forty-six, if you factor in how he probably didn't even want to go. I can't decide whether I'm touched at his sweetness or, once again, baffled by his stupidity.

"*Uh, Joy?*" Noah whispers to me uncomfortably as the strains of some synthesized Barry medley start playing overhead. "*Is it okay if I get kind of . . . cozy with you?*"

"*What?*" I don't mean to sound as startled as I probably do.

"*It's just . . .*" Noah is leaning in closer to me now, and I can smell the root beer barrel in his mouth. "*You know how these chairs don't have any armrests? Well, the woman next to me is taking up her chair, plus two-thirds of mine.*"

I glance over, and there he is, looking all tight with

Fanny Pack Lady. I can tell he's trying to take up as little room as possible, sitting up straight and crunching his arms near his chest, but her midsection oozes onto him anyway. I can't help shuddering.

"Yeah, no problem. Cozy up to me all you want." I have a decent amount of room on my other side, since the old man next to me parked his walker at the entrance. He's a pretty small guy, so I scootch over as far as I can and feel Noah exhale on the other side of me.

"Thanks," he whispers again. His breath tickles from the top of my cheek to my bottom lip. I can feel the warmth of him next to me. His warmth is more than warmth: It's the warmth, and it's the pressure of him against me, and it's knowing he's there, so close to me. All of it swirls together to make this fantastic, better-than-warm feeling wrap around my insides. I'm all about to get caught up in it when Barry takes the stage, and I just get warmer and warmer.

I mean, it's not Barry, obviously. It's some guy made up to look like Barry, but as impersonators go, this guy is incredible. He has this ageless face—kind of plastic, like the faces of the animatronic statues in Caesars Palace. It's a face that makes it impossible to tell how old he really is. His hair is cut spiky-short, and he's wearing Barry's signature swanky white jacket with satin lapels.

"*Spooky,*" whispers Noah, mesmerized. His breath tickles my ear and makes me laugh.

"*What's so funny?*" Noah says low into my ear. There's laughter in his voice.

"*Nothing,*" I say, soaking in his closeness, his warmness, the Barry before me.

I can't remember the last time I felt this kind of good. I'm not sure I've *ever* felt this kind of good. It's not excited anticipation. It's not something as vague as hope or as in-your-face as delight. It's just pure good.

I am hyperaware of Noah next to me, our bodies touching from shoulder to thigh. Each place he touches zaps and sizzles with this all-natural kind of electricity. It's this amazing electricity I've never felt before, and if we could only figure out how to run the world with it, going green wouldn't be hard at all.

And I know this man on the stage isn't Barry Manilow, but it's easy to forget as he launches into "It's a Miracle," with a dead-on Barry smile. And I know this boy next to me isn't my boyfriend, but it's easy to forget as the natural electricity dissolves any trace of ice-blood from my system.

BARRY SONGS THAT
REMIND ME OF NOAH

"Could It Be Magic"

"I Made It Through the Rain"

"Ready to Take a Chance Again"

READY TO TAKE A
CHANCE AGAIN

I know what's going to happen even before I unfold my arms and rest my left hand on my thigh. I don't have any practice at Haven-style flirting, but somehow it comes as natural as breathing. I move my hand about a centimeter toward Noah.

He moves his hand about a centimeter toward me. Then he covers my little finger with his. We're not holding hands yet—we're holding pinkies. But it's enough to send a fresh surge of natural electricity though my body, stopping to energize all my core areas. After about thirty seconds, when he moves his entire hand over mine—his entire not-too-soft-not-too-rough hand—it feels warm and perfect and right.

I look up, and Barry's crooning away, and he starts up with "Mandy." My favorite. In fourth grade, when I had to grow a spider plant for a science project, I named mine Mandy and played her nothing but that song, over and over. It's a song I know better than by heart. It's a song that's inside of me, and hearing it here, live, all around, I drink it in.

Then it happens. Barry pauses just a few beats too long between the third and fourth measure of the first verse. It startles me so much that Noah looks over at me, worried. "Are you okay?" I see his mouth move more than I hear his words. He starts to move his hand away from mine, but I lead it back to me.

A million thoughts are swirling in my head and I can't finish thinking any of them. But I nod. I nod because I'm better than okay. I nod because this, just now, this is a revelation. And maybe, just maybe, this was the reason God left me stranded with Noah in Las Vegas.

This man up onstage is not Barry Manilow. He has made me believe that he is Barry Manilow so fully that it is only when he makes a mistake that I realize he isn't. In this performance he's a Barry Manilow cardboard cutout. But in real life, when this show ends, he will go back to being himself—whoever that is. Maybe sometimes we're all impersonating someone, trying to be a cutout because it's less complicated than being who we really are.

Maybe Zan was right, in a way—not about everybody else, but about me. Maybe it was easier for me to be a cutout of Zan's girlfriend—hating Haven, hating the Soccer Lovin' Kids, for no real reason other than Zan hating them, too.

This man in front of us is more than a guy who's a Barry Manilow cutout five afternoons a week. I am more than Zan's girlfriend. Noah's more than a Soccer Lovin' Kid. We're all just us, just people, free to make our lives as real and as complicated as we want to.

I curl my fingers around Noah's fingers. I relax into him. For the first time I can remember, I can think my thoughts all the way through.

For the first time I can remember, I relax.

CLOSURE

When we get up to leave the theater, Noah doesn't let go of my hand. I don't know why holding hands while standing up feels different than holding hands while sitting down, but it does. It makes me tingle with that pure happiness. I feel another tingle, too, though—one I recognize. It's not from Noah. I need to go to the bathroom.

I hate public restrooms, and I hate trying to find one in this crazy place even more, but I don't have much of a choice. "Can we find a restroom?" I ask Noah, and he nods.

"We passed one on the way in," he says, smiling. Discussing restroom whereabouts isn't usually smile-inducing, but his smile makes me smile back at him. Maybe he's glad we're not talking about how tightly we're holding hands, glad I'm not getting all relationshippy on him. We're not at Haven High now—nobody to see us, nobody to ask us if Noah's going to be the first Soccer

Lovin' Kid to have a girlfriend. We can take our time figuring out what this all means. After all, we have a six-hour drive ahead of us.

It's when I'm in one of the surprisingly nice marble stalls getting out a toilet seat cover that I remember that bathroom at Haven High, three weeks ago. Hiding from Noah. My life up to leaving on the trip plays in fast-forward. The scenes in my mind are mostly of Mattia, and I know I need to finally talk to her. It's time.

I empty my bladder at lightning speed and the toilet flushes beneath me. Even though I do up my jeans, I don't leave the stall. I need some privacy for this call.

It doesn't feel like a Sunday, but it is. Mattia has the early church schedule—nine to noon. She'll definitely be back by now. Part of me is afraid she'll let it go to voice mail, but I have to at least try. She answers on the second ring. "Hey. Are you back?"

I can't read her tone. Mattia's master of the poker face, and she has the voice to go along with it. "No, not yet. We got . . . delayed. Noah's car broke down, but it's all good now."

"Good." Mattia pauses. "So . . . did it go . . . well?" She says it slowly, like she's second-guessing every word.

"Yeah. I found Zan." I deliberate about telling her the next part. "He has a new girlfriend. Ismene."

"Ismene? What in the heck kind of name is that?" The old Mattia is back. "I mean, seriously? Could you *be* more pretentious?"

"It's from *Antigone*. You know, her sister?"

Mattia scoffs. "Whatever. Antigone's sister's name is 'is-meanie.' Not ease-men." Some people might write poetry about the wasted minds of Haven High, but Mattia's is not one of them. Mattia may be a pop-psychology-loving social butterfly, but she's smart, too, and she tells it like it is. "This girl sounds like the world's biggest poseur."

There's a long pause, and I wonder if I'm supposed to say something. Is this when I apologize?

"I'm sorry, though." Mattia's voice is softer. "That he's got a new girlfriend. That you couldn't get . . . closure."

"I'm not sure that closure exists. Not in real life, at least. But I think I got my own kind of closure."

"Did you finally realize you're too good for him?"

"No, that's not it. I think I realized that he's not too good for me."

She pauses. "Okay, I'm way too tired to figure out what that means. You're going to have to explain it to me."

I grab another toilet seat cover and sit down. "Well, it's like I always thought Zan was perfect. Genius-smart, Abercrombie-handsome—"

Mattia snorts.

"Like he was a step above everybody else in Haven. No offense."

"Oh, no worries, none taken." But a smile is creeping into her voice, I can tell.

"Coming here, I realized something, though. I thought he was better than everybody else; he thought he was better than everybody else. But he isn't."

"Nope," says Mattia, like it's been clear to her all the time. "He's worse."

"You're missing the point! He's not better or worse. Nobody is. We're all just people."

"Yep," Mattia says, like this, too, has been clear to her all the time.

So maybe it's just me, getting it for the first time. "Listen, I guess what it comes down to is that I'm not Zan's girlfriend anymore—and I'm good with that. It's like, before I thought I couldn't be myself without him. But I can. In some ways it's easier." I don't realize I know these things until I say them to her. Now I can be more than Zan's girlfriend. I don't have to spend my life trying to get back to Joy 2.0. I can just be me.

"Anyway, I'm sorry that I've been so wrapped up in what I lost that I haven't seen what I have. Which is a dang good friend like you."

"Dang good," says Mattia. "But you're a dang good

friend, too. And I'm sorry for not being more supportive. I just wanted you to be happy, and Zan . . . you never seemed that happy with him. You just seemed happy that he wanted to be with you."

I was. But that was before. "It's different now." I think of Noah.

"Yeah, I know it is. I can tell. Non sequitur: Will you be back tonight?"

"Uh-huh. I'll text you when I get in, okay?"

"Okay. Take care."

"You too."

BACK WHEN YOU
WERE EASIER TO LOVE

It occurs to me when I stand up to flush the second toilet seat cover. But the walls of these stalls are marble; too nice to deface. Besides, I don't have a Sharpie. I dig around in my purse to see what I do have, and there are my sticky-notes from the Lucky Seven. So I grab a pen and write, "Back when you were easier to love." Then I tear off the note and post it right on the swinging door.

LEAVING LAS VEGAS

Noah and I hold hands as we walk out to the SAAB, and his hand brushes mine when we stop at red lights. When we stop to fill up the car we walk out of the convenience store holding hands—and jumbo-size cups of Sprite.

And in real life, I am so lucky. In real life, "Copacabana" is playing on the tape deck, and Noah is joining in with me on the chorus.